BRIGHT SPARKS

A clever Scottish mystery that keeps you guessing

TRAUDE AILINGER

Published by The Book Folks

London, 2023

This book is a work of fiction. Names, characters, businesses, organizations, places and events are either the product of the author's imagination or are used fictitiously. Any resemblance to actual persons, living or dead, events or locales is entirely coincidental. The spelling is British English.

ISBN 978-1-80462-128-8

www.thebookfolks.com

BRIGHT SPARKS is the fifth book in a series of amateur sleuth mystery titles set in Edinburgh. For details about the other books in the series, head to the back of this one.

Prologue

At last, I've got hold of a good one. Not a rickety garden shed or an old banger for me this time; no, a proper mansion. Even though it's difficult, I'm savouring the moment, prolonging the pleasure. Slow licks along the carpet, around the curved legs of a mahogany desk and up the curtains to the delicately moulded cornices on the ceiling. Books are my favourite – especially old, wonderfully dry first editions – but there are only a few newspapers and magazines here to fuel my passion. I'm not so keen on flesh; my eternal foe is made into solid lumps that simply won't catch until I've turned the whole room into an inferno. The smaller body downstairs puts up less resistance than the one on the first floor, though even that eventually shrinks into a contorted boxer's pose as a last act of defiance against the inevitable.

Reaching through the bursting windows, I wave triumphantly at the gawping neighbours and my arch enemies who are already approaching with their pathetic hoses as if they could stop me now. I know they'll defeat me in the end, but until then, I'll fight them all the way.

Chapter 1

Detective Inspector Russell McCord surveyed the charred walls of the ironically named Roseburn House in the upmarket Murrayfield area of Edinburgh and reflected – with some degree of *schadenfreude*, it has to be said – on the fragile fortunes even of the rich. Thanks to their solid stone structure, the outer walls of the Edwardian mansion were still standing, but the once gleaming windows had turned into blackened holes, their original symmetry smudged by soot. The tiled roof had collapsed with the few remaining blackened beams pointing into the clear blue sky as if begging a higher power to take pity. The sweet fragrance of honeysuckle and lavender that had greeted McCord at the gate had given way to a lingering smell of acrid smoke that hung over the ruin like a toxic blanket.

For the past few days, the city had been lazing in a balmy twenty-five degrees, and not a breath of air was stirring the majestic trees dotted throughout the extensive garden.

As a true Scot, McCord considered this kind of weather a heatwave. He was desperate to take off his jacket but did not want to look unprofessional in front of the fire investigator who, clad in a protective overall, looked like an oversized astronaut exploring an ash-covered planet. His friendly blue eyes scrutinised the much shorter detective in a cheap but immaculate suit.

"You must be DI McCord," the fire investigator said. "I'm Bill Reid."

He peeled off a glove to shake hands, but realising that he was grimy and sweaty, he pulled back with an apologetic smile. "It's like an oven in there."

"You have found a body?" McCord asked. He liked people to come straight to the point.

"Two, to be precise," Reid said, pulling a handkerchief from his pocket to wipe his flushed, shiny face.

McCord raised his dark eyebrows. "I was only told about one."

Reid nodded. "One human, one cat. The latter might well have been the arsonist."

"What do you mean?"

McCord did not like being presented with riddles, nor was he a particularly patient man – although he tried, at least with strangers.

Reid happily seized the opportunity to explain.

"We think the fire started in the living room. We found a melted ashtray on the floor and the remains of what is probably a cat next to it. Maybe the ashtray had a burning cigarette or cigar in it and moggy knocked it over. It wouldn't be the first time a fire was caused by a careless smoker."

McCord grew increasingly irritated. "You think the fire was an accident? Then why was I called out here? To arrest a barbecued pussycat for arson?"

"I asked Mr Reid to call you because I don't believe it was an accident," a familiar voice sounded behind him.

McCord swivelled round to face Amy Thornton, journalist and self-declared investigator of any murder she decided to stick her long nose in. McCord's heart skipped a beat at the sight of her large, dark eyes and mischievous smile. It was more than three months since their last case together and he had begun to doubt she would be back in his life at all. Yet here she was; still beautiful, still irritating as hell.

"I should have known," McCord said with a theatrical sigh. "Where there's a body, there's Miss Thornton with a wild theory. Who do you think I should arrest this time – the cat's jilted lover? Or the neighbour's dog perhaps?"

Amy shook her head, which made her dark ponytail swing violently to and fro. "Don't be facetious, McCord," she said, "and think this through for a moment. Do you really think a cat would just sit there and watch a fire spread without at least trying to run away? Especially since the window was open."

Amy looked to Reid for confirmation.

"That is true," he said.

McCord shrugged. "I'm no expert in feline psychology, but you might have a point."

"Of course, I do," Amy said. "But because of your obsession with the cat, you seem to have forgotten that there was another body. That of a human."

"Do we know who it is?" McCord asked Reid, who was following the conversation with great interest.

"Not yet. You'll need dental records or a DNA sample to make a positive identification. But Miss Thornton here thinks she knows who the victim is."

"Of course she does," McCord said and turned to Amy. "Are you going to tell me, or shall we play a guessing game to while away the morning?"

"Victoria Norval, CEO of BSeen, a successful marketing company, recently much involved in the fashion industry," Amy said without rising to the bait. "She lived here with her husband, Morton Fisher, and his son, Patrick. No one has seen her since the fire, and there has been no social media activity on her accounts either."

"There could be any number of reasons for that. Anything else?" McCord asked.

"There are a lot of people who will be glad that she's dead."

Just how Amy was able to sniff out people's private relationships was a mystery to McCord, although he would never have admitted that to her.

"And you know this how?" he asked.

"I happened to be waiting at a red light on Queensferry Road when I heard about it on Forth 1 radio. Since I was in the neighbourhood anyway, I drove straight here. Naturally, I was curious to find out what had happened."

"Naturally," McCord said drily. "And when you arrived, you found several people jumping up and down with joy?"

"Not exactly," Amy said. "But the whole family was here, not only Morton Fisher and his son, but also Fisher's daughter, Danielle. They were all clearly more distressed about the state of the house than concerned about Norval's well-being. They seemed to think she had taken off somewhere, and I overheard Patrick, the son, saying that it was probably her who had set the house on fire. But if that's true, whose body is in there? All the other family members are accounted for."

"Do we know where this loving family is to be found now?" McCord asked.

"They're staying at The Braemar. When the fire broke out, they were all at the husband's sixtieth birthday party. Well, everybody apart from Norval and her killer."

"Easy now," McCord said with a side glance to Reid, who was listening raptly. "Let's not spread rumours that could leave us with a defamation suit. So, Mr Reid, we'll leave you to get on with your work. Let me know when forensics can go in and I'll send them over. I'd like your report as soon as possible, please."

Reid nodded and pulled up his face mask as he re-entered the building.

McCord turned to Amy. A man more in tune with the other sex would have made a casual remark suggesting a cool drink in this hot weather, but not McCord. "What are you up to then?" he asked instead.

"An interview in Marchmont," Amy said, checking the time on her phone, "and I'm already late. Bye!"

McCord watched her as she rushed towards the road, her flowery cotton dress undulating around her petite frame. How she managed to move so fast on high heels was something else McCord could not fathom, but there were so many things he did not understand about Amy Thornton, he had given up trying.

He was secretly relieved that she had left so quickly as her unexpected appearance had caught him completely off guard. They had not seen each other since that disastrous dinner at a Japanese restaurant in February. Why on earth had he agreed to go to a place where you had to sit cross-legged on the floor and eat miso soup? Because it had been Amy's idea and at that moment, he would have gone anywhere she suggested. He had made a valiant effort to pretend that he was enjoying himself, but his face had involuntarily contorted when he bit on a slimy piece of raw tuna. He would have much preferred the famous Kobe steak, but its price tag had made him choke. When Amy reprimanded him for his lack of culinary sophistication, he had gasped with a sudden pain of cramp in his legs, hauled himself off the cushion he was sitting on and hobbled ignominiously towards the exit.

After that performance, Amy had given up on the charms of the Far East and taken off in a huff, while McCord had picked up the horrendous bill and then gone for a curry from the Taj Mahal, which he had eaten alone in front of the telly.

Despite the unmitigated disaster that had been their first real date, he had been confident that the next murder would send Amy scurrying to St Leonard's police station, but neither a bloodbath in Craigmillar nor the attempted assassination of a local councillor had brought her back. Eventually, he had been so concerned that he had swallowed his pride and phoned John Campbell, Amy's boss at *Forth Write* magazine, only to be told that Amy had been on several assignments abroad and would continue to be for the next couple of months.

McCord would not have been DI McCord, the by now famous detective, had he failed to pick up on the embarrassment in John Campbell's genteel voice, but he had also, and just as typically, drawn the wrong conclusion and assumed that Amy was going to considerable lengths to avoid his company. He had faithfully bought the magazine each week, flicking through her articles about the great fashion houses of Paris, London, Milan and Amsterdam. With some bewilderment, he had viewed the pictures of skinny models wearing wholly impractical clothes and scanned the text in between for evidence of some infatuation beyond fashion, local architecture and food.

But now she was back, and the first thing she did was make him look like a fool in front of the fire investigation officer.

With an exasperated sigh, he took a walk in the beautiful garden, stretching at least fifty yards to Ravelston Dykes Road. The high wall surrounding the property muffled the traffic noise to a soothing hum and turned the place into an oasis of calm. He took off his jacket and rested his slim, wiry frame against the trunk of an old sycamore. Bees and wasps were buzzing around the heads of red clover peeking out from the lush grass that was dappled with spots of sunlight. A blackbird was pulling a worm from the soil of a flowerbed.

He imagined living here instead of his cramped flat in Portobello and riled once more against the gulf between the haves and the have-nots in this country. But then he remembered the burnt-out shell behind him and the family rifts that Amy had hinted at, and cautioned himself to be careful what he wished for.

As McCord walked along the path, he had the strangest feeling of being watched. He looked around but could not see anybody until a rustling sound drew his attention to the ground. A girl of no more than eighteen in a green gardener's smock was kneeling in front of a flowerbed concealed by one of the many rose bushes that probably had given the house its name. Next to her lay half a dozen pots of lavender plants and a large watering can. She held a soil-encrusted trowel suspended in the air as he stopped to speak to her.

"Hi, I'm DI McCord. Who are you?"

"I'm Chloe."

"Chloe?"

"Chalmers. Pleased to meet you."

She made no move to get up.

"And you," McCord said, surprised. Most people did not profess to being pleased when they were accosted by an officer of the law.

Chloe Chalmers lowered her eyes to the ground and with an assured movement drove the trowel into the damp, crumbling earth, digging a square hole of what seemed a very precise perimeter and depth. Gently, she lifted one of the small lavender bushes out of its pot and lowered it into the hole. It fitted perfectly. With her bare hands, she patted down the earth around the plant and watered it generously.

"The fire engines have made a right mess of the garden," McCord said, pointing to the broad tyre tracks cutting through the well-kept lawn and its colourful borders, leaving a trail of destruction.

Chalmers kept her head down.

"Yes," she said quietly. "I hate to see the garden like this."

She wiped the sweat off her forehead with the sleeve of the blue T-shirt she was wearing under her smock, leaving a brown mark, which she either did not notice or ignored. Her face had the pale and freckled complexion of a redhead, but her hair was hidden under a dotted, blue-and-white headscarf. Normally, the women he spoke to made an effort to impress, but this girl couldn't care less.

She had already moved along a few yards and begun to dig a second hole. McCord followed her slowly, watching her with fascination.

"Did you know that it has been scientifically proven that contact with the soil lowers your heart rate?" She looked up at him with striking green eyes and smiled. "You should try it sometime. You seem very tense."

As if to prove the point, she took a handful of the rich, dark soil and let it run through her hands as if it were caressing her.

McCord's first instinct was to tell her that he was not tense at all and to mind her own business, but he had to admit that she was right. He was tense. Hardly surprising, with a charred body lying less than thirty yards away in the smouldering ruin of a five-million-pound mansion.

"Want to plant one?"

Chalmers held up the trowel, but McCord shook his head. "I go birdwatching," he said.

She nodded, and McCord saw that she understood.

"Do you know the family well?" he asked.

Chalmers shrugged.

"Not really. Victoria, eh, Ms Norval employed me to rewild part of the garden at the back. She was really into it and when she was home, she often came out to chat to me."

"Have you seen her since the fire by any chance?"

Chalmers frowned. "Who did you say you were?"

McCord pulled out his ID and flipped it open with practised ease.

"Detective Inspector McCord, Edinburgh CID, Homicide Division."

Chalmers dropped her trowel.

"Homicide? This was just an accidental fire, wasn't it?"

"That is possible," McCord said, "but a body has been found inside."

Chalmers stared at McCord, her face horror-stricken. "There was somebody in the house?" she whispered. "And you think it was her? Ms Norval?"

"We don't know yet," McCord said. "The family seem to think that she was somewhere else. Do you know where she might be?"

"I have no idea. She did not confide in me, but I had the strong impression that she was not very happy here."

"What makes you say that?" McCord asked.

"I never heard her speak to the others in a friendly way. Either they were arguing, or they were giving each other the silent treatment. Once she came out to me and asked if I had some wood that needed chopping because otherwise, she might take an axe to somebody's head. We laughed, and then she helped me build the bug hotel."

"Do you have any idea what happened here on Saturday night?" McCord asked.

Chalmers shook her head. "They were all out to celebrate Mr Fisher's sixtieth birthday."

"And you were not invited?"

"Of course not. It was a very posh affair, I should imagine."

"So, who lived in the house at the time of the fire?" McCord asked.

"Mr Fisher, Ms Norval, and Mr Fisher's son, Patrick, from his first marriage. His daughter Danielle McLellan, also by his first wife, and his grandson Hunter were here, but they were only visiting; and then there was Jennifer Hamill, the housekeeper."

"Where were the two of you during the fire?"

"I was out for a walk on the golf course," Chalmers said, "and Jennifer was at the theatre." She lowered her head. "If we'd stayed here, we could have saved whoever was in there, couldn't we?"

"We don't know that. There is no point in torturing yourself," McCord said.

Keeping her eyes on the purple shrub, she asked, "Did they suffer?"

McCord shook his head. "Fire victims tend to die of the fumes, sometimes even in their sleep, before the flames reach them."

"You're not saying that in order to make me feel better, are you?" There was suspicion in her voice.

"We have to wait for the fire investigator to submit his report to be sure," McCord explained, "but that's what usually happens. A small consolation, but at least something."

"Yes, at least something," she echoed.

"We'll need a formal statement from you," McCord said. "Could you come into St Leonard's police station in the next couple of days? There is nothing to worry about," he added, seeing that she was not keen on the idea. "It won't take long."

"There is so much to do here," she said. "But I'll come, of course."

"Thank you," McCord said.

He turned towards the ruin. "You didn't stay at the house? It seems big enough."

She twisted her upper body and pointed to the tiny cottage crouching next to Roseburn House. Miraculously, it had been spared by the fire.

"At least you haven't lost your home," McCord said.

Chalmers did not reply. She seemed absorbed in the task of lowering the next plant into the ground.

"Goodbye," McCord said, surprised to find that he would have liked to stay a little longer.

Chalmers glanced up at him.

"Bye," she said and went back to her task.

Chapter 2

McCord decided to walk the few hundred yards to The Braemar Hotel, an imposing Victorian pile not far from the Chinese Consulate on Corstorphine Road. Its garden stretched down to the Water of Leith, which winds its way from the Pentland Hills to middle-class Balerno and Currie, past council houses in Saughton until it reaches Roseburn where the upper echelons of Edinburgh society reside. Quite unimpressed, it then continues its course past Stockbridge through the north of the city until it reaches Leith and eventually joins the Firth of Forth.

After pushing his ID right up to the supercilious manager's nose, McCord was reluctantly admitted to the second-floor suite currently inhabited by Mr Morton Fisher, whose bulging waistline and red face identified him as a man who consumed too much alcohol and too much red meat – in fact, too much of everything. He wore a polo shirt with a logo McCord did not recognise but, he suspected, indicated a hefty price tag, and chino shorts that revealed fat and hairy legs, so far untouched by the sun.

He seemed to have recovered well from the shock of losing his home and, one way or the other, his wife; this was possibly helped by the contents of a bottle of Prince Hubert de Polignac VSOP cognac sitting on the glass-topped coffee table next to an empty snifter. Fisher, noticing the detective's glance, seemed torn between a welcome opportunity to brag and a strong desire not to share the liquid gold with the hoi polloi. After a brief inner struggle, the need to impress won, and Fisher lifted a clean balloon glass from the sideboard.

"A little soupçon?" he asked.

Instead of an answer, McCord merely shook his head. He had not been in Fisher's company for two minutes and he already disliked his host intensely, fighting back the impulse to punch the arrogant sod. He wished he had asked his partner, DS Duncan Calderwood, to come with him, but he was back at St Leonard's, using what he had hoped would be a quiet Sunday duty to catch up with his paperwork. Hailing from old money and born with impeccable manners, Calderwood spoke the language of the rich and powerful, and always managed to say the right thing. Ach, to hell, he thought.

"I need to ask you a few questions about the fire at Roseburn House."

"I really don't know why you should bother," Fisher said, squeezing himself into a tartan-covered armchair, leaving McCord to stand. "Some fire investigator is no doubt raking through the ashes as we speak. Damn shame. But then, the insurance will have to cough up, and I can finally put underfloor heating in. Did you know I once owned an insurance company?"

"I didn't," McCord admitted. "It would be ironic if you had insured your own house and it burnt down, wouldn't it?"

The veins in Fisher's skin seemed to expand into a network of purple rivulets. "Unlike you, I don't see the funny side of this at all."

"Neither do I," McCord said sharply, "especially since a dead body has been found inside the house. Do you have any idea who that might be?"

There was a brief pause.

"There must be a mistake," Fisher said, his voice betraying no emotion. "During the fire, we were all at Dine Murrayfield to celebrate my sixtieth birthday. The family, that is, and a few friends. When we heard about the fire, we rushed back, but all we could do was watch the fire brigade failing to get it under control. Useless they were. Later in the evening, I spoke to Jennifer, our housekeeper, and the gardener girl, what's her name again... Zoe?"

"Chloe," McCord said, in an unsuccessful attempt to keep the censure out of his voice. But he need not have bothered; it did not even register with Fisher.

"Anyway, they were both very much alive."

"What about your wife? I have it on good authority that she has not been seen since the fire and hasn't posted on social media either. Are you not concerned at all about her?" McCord asked.

"I have no reason to be concerned. She chose the party to announce that she hated us all and would be leaving." He sat up and poured himself another cognac. "The fire was probably caused by some junkie who broke in and was then too wasted to find his way out." Fisher swirled the amber liquid around his glass. "I'm sorry I can't help you any further."

The problem was that he did not look sorry at all.

McCord was of a mind to stay and keep asking Fisher questions until his precious cognac had evaporated, but he doubted he would get anywhere with him before the identity of the body was confirmed.

"I'd like to speak to the other members of your family," McCord said. "You have a son and a daughter? Are they staying here at the hotel as well?"

"Unfortunately for my bank account, yes," Fisher replied. "They're out in the garden. We don't get many days like this in Scotland."

"How come you haven't joined them?" McCord asked.

Fisher took a sip of his cognac and sloshed it round in his mouth before he swallowed noisily. "Do you have children, DI...?"

"McCord. No, I don't."

"If you did, you would know that children only want you around when there is something in it for them. Right now, they'll be whingeing about having lost all their possessions. Patrick will claim that a literary masterpiece has been destroyed; don't believe a word of it. He fancies himself as an undiscovered Pulitzer Prize winner, but I couldn't get his God-awful book published even when I called in a favour from an old friend in the industry."

"Thank you for that background information," McCord said in a neutral voice. "I'll have a word with them now."

Fisher looked at him, full of contempt. "I thought Edinburgh CID would have better things to do than waste time and manpower investigating accidents," he said, "but if it keeps you all in a job... Goodbye, Inspector."

He did not bother to get up from his chair.

McCord turned on his heel and left without a word.

* * *

The Braemar prided itself not only on the style and comfort of its hotel rooms, but also on the beautifully laid-out garden where the illustrious guests could go for a stroll after their exquisite four-course lunches or dinners in order to make room for the next meal.

Walking between carefully manicured lawns and flowerbeds, where someone must have used a ruler to measure the distance between the begonias, McCord discovered that the hotel had not one, not two, but three different patio areas, all sheltered from curious glances by trellises covered in blooming clematis. As he quietly approached patio number three, he heard a plaintive male voice declaring, "If you ask me, *she* did it, the spiteful cow, and then she got a fright and disappeared."

"Sh!" somebody hissed, "don't say things like that, and especially not with Hunter around. You know what he's like."

The man laughed. "Yes, Sis, I know. He leaves a trail of destruction wherever he goes, but that young man will go far."

Confident that he had found the Fisher family, McCord decided to use the offended silence that followed to walk round the trellis.

A casually dressed man in his mid-thirties and a heavily made-up woman who was trying to look much younger but failing miserably, were sitting at a glass-topped wicker table and drinking colourful cocktails with little umbrellas that reminded McCord of a night out in town with an aftermath he rather wanted to forget.

A little further down the slope, a boy of about nine was constructing a bow from a branch and a piece of string. He held a large Swiss Army Knife in his small hands, vigorously cutting a notch into the wood. McCord worried about the safety of it but, having no experience of young children, he decided that it was up to the other adults to intervene.

"Detective Inspector McCord, Edinburgh CID. Could I have a word?"

The two adults, startled, froze in their seats. The boy immediately dropped the knife, whose blade missed his naked foot by a hair's breadth, and ran up to McCord.

"You are the famous detective! The one who got shot! Can I see your scar?" His bright blue eyes were shining with excitement.

"No," McCord said curtly.

"Will you give me an autograph?"

"No!"

Undeterred, the boy continued his questioning.

"Who has been murdered?"

"Hunter, shush, mind your manners!" the woman scolded him.

The man, laughing, rose from his chair. "Patrick Fisher. This is my sister, Danielle McLellan, and this splendid young man here is Hunter, my nephew." He pointed to the empty chair. "Please have a seat. How can we help you, Inspector?"

But McCord turned to the boy instead. "What makes you think there has been a murder?" he asked.

Hunter shrugged. "Well," he said in the patient tone of an adult who explains the obvious to a slow-witted child, "you are a homicide detective, and homicide means murder, so somebody must have been murdered. Grandpa's wife has disappeared, and nobody liked her, so I think she's been murdered. But it wasn't me."

"Hunter!" Danielle McLellan raised her hands in despair. "I must apologise for my son's behaviour, Inspector. I don't know what's got into him today. It must be the heat and all the excitement about the fire."

Patrick Fisher laughed again. "Hunter is a very... confident child, but he does live in his own little universe. I assume you want to talk to us about the house fire, Inspector?"

McCord nodded. "Yes, but unfortunately, not only that. When the fire investigator was finally able to enter the building this morning, a body was found. Because of the circumstances, we are treating the death as suspicious."

Patrick Fisher and his sister exchanged a look that McCord found difficult to interpret.

"Strictly speaking, there were two bodies," he added. "And the second one was not human but the remains of a cat."

"A cat?" Hunter edged ever closer to McCord until he was right at his elbow.

"Hunter!" His mother's voice had taken on a shrill tone. "Please go to your room. You can play on your iPad if you like," she added seductively.

"No, I want to stay here. This is much more interesting," Hunter declared, not moving an inch.

"A body?" Patrick Fisher asked, slowly putting down the Bloody Mary he had been sipping. "No way. Who could that be?"

"That's what I was going to ask you," McCord said. "Do you happen to know where your stepmother is? Apparently, she has not been seen or heard of since the fire."

"Victoria?" Patrick Fisher laughed, but this time without mirth. "She's run off with her boyfriend. And before you ask, no, I don't know who her boyfriend is, and I don't want to know either. Good riddance if you ask me."

"Did she tell you that she was going to see him?" McCord asked.

"She told everybody that she hated us all and that she was leaving," Danielle McLellan butted in. "And she said that to the whole family, also in the presence of Daddy's friends, and to top it all, during his birthday party! I've never seen him so angry and upset. What kind of person does a thing like that?"

"A person who is drunk and doesn't care about anybody but herself," Patrick Fisher said. "She married Dad for his money, and when she managed to reel in a younger man, she was off."

"How do you know it is a younger man if you don't know who he is?" McCord asked.

"Because... because..." Patrick Fisher stammered, "I don't *know*, I just assumed that was the case because she is a lot younger than Dad."

"Right," McCord said, not even pretending to believe him. "Can you tell me what exactly happened at this birthday party? It was held at a restaurant near here, wasn't it?"

"Yes, the Dine Murrayfield," Danielle McLellan said, diverting McCord's attention away from her blundering brother. "Not quite Daddy's style but a very nice place. It's close enough to walk from the house, so we could all have a drink." She laughed. "Quite a few drinks, actually. Anyway, we had cocktails and then a buffet dinner. Daddy made a very nice speech about how important family is and how wonderful it was to have everybody he cared about together, and then she, Victoria, grunted – like a pig, I thought at the time. She stood up and said she could not stand one more minute of his hypocrisy, and that tomorrow she would make everybody see what a despicable human being he was." Danielle McLellan was trembling with rage at the memory.

"What did she mean by that?" McCord asked. "It sounds as if she was going to unveil some sort of secret."

"The woman was off her head," Danielle McLellan spat. "Daddy doesn't have any secrets."

McCord noticed the trace of a condescending smile around Patrick Fisher's lips. "Do you know of anything that Ms Norval might have wanted to reveal?"

The smile vanished.

"Absolutely not," Patrick Fisher said. "If you ask me, she felt she needed to say something to justify her leaving Dad."

"And who do you think the body in the house might be if it is not your stepmother?" McCord asked, looking at both the adults in turn for an answer.

"I have no idea," Danielle McLellan said. "What a horrible thought, somebody dying in there, in the flames, while we were standing outside." She shuddered.

"I understand you all returned to Roseburn House when you heard about the fire?" McCord asked.

"Yes, one of the staff at the hotel, who knows where we live, read about the fire on social media and told Dad," Patrick Fisher said. "We all hurried home and found the house in flames. It was a complete inferno. We were all in shock. We still are."

"Did either of you or the other guests leave before the fire?" McCord asked.

Patrick Fisher frowned. "What do you mean?"

"He means, could anybody at the party have set the house on fire," Hunter piped up. "He wants to know if we all have an alibi."

Patrick Fisher stared at McCord. "You're not suggesting that any of us... this is crazy! Why would we burn down our family home? We lost all our personal belongings, stuff that no insurance can replace. My latest novel, for example–"

"I'm sure you have a copy on iCloud," Danielle McLellan said dismissively. She obviously shared her father's contempt for her brother's literary efforts. "But Patrick is right," she continued, turning to McCord. "Why would we? It was a terrible accident. If there was a person inside, it must have been a burglar."

"That's what your father suggested as well," McCord said. "But the restaurant is only a ten-minute walk from Roseburn House. With all the guests milling around, somebody could have slipped away, set fire to the house, and come back unnoticed."

"No, they couldn't," Patrick Fisher said angrily. "We were all there, chatting about the bombshell Victoria had dropped."

"Your father as well? You said he was very upset."

"Grandpa was furious," Hunter said. "His face turned purple, and he ran out of the room – I've never seen him move so fast! I think he went into the garden because he didn't want everybody staring at him."

"Hunter!" his mother exclaimed again. "One more word, and I'll take you to your room myself!"

"There's no need," McCord said. "I think I have enough information to get on with. But I might have to speak to you again. Please notify St Leonard's police station should you plan to check out of the hotel."

With that, he turned to go and made his way back to the driveway. He had walked no more than a few yards when he realised that he was being followed. He pretended not to notice, and sure enough, less than a minute later, Hunter appeared at his side.

"What was it you said about a cat in the fire?" he asked McCord.

McCord hesitated. He shouldn't really talk about the investigation, but then, it was only a cat, and Hunter was just a child. A child that had already given him some valuable insight into the workings of this family.

"The remains of a cat were found on the floor next to an ashtray where they think the fire started. The window was open, so the cat probably got in and knocked over the ashtray that had a burning cigarette or cigar in it."

Hunter was silent for some time and McCord wondered if the terrible fate of the animal had affected the boy more than the presumed death of his grandfather's wife.

"I'm sorry," McCord said, "but you don't need to worry. The fire investigator said it would not have suffered."

Hunter gave him a disappointed look. "Don't treat me like a stupid child," he told McCord. "How would you like to choke to death on poisonous gases?"

"Not much," McCord admitted, "sorry." He wasn't sure why he felt he should apologise to a nine-year-old, but there he was.

"No worries, guv," Hunter said graciously. "But something is not kosher about that stiff. I've got a hunch, but I need to check something out first. I'll get back to you. See you later, alligator."

He then turned back towards the house.

McCord wondered if he should tell the boy's mother to check what her son was watching on the internet, but he had the impression that Hunter always did exactly what he wanted to do anyway. And, to his surprise, he found that he looked forward to seeing that boy again.

* * *

Back at St Leonard's police station, DS Duncan Calderwood had already put up an incident board with printed-out photos of the members of the Fisher family surrounding the picture of an attractive blonde woman in her early forties. The caption underneath said 'Victoria Norval – victim?'

"Is this not a little premature?" McCord asked his partner, who had taken off his tailor-made jacket and was pinning notes with information on the people on the board. "We don't even know yet if a crime has been committed, nor who the victim is. And come to think of it, how do you know about what... Of course, silly me. Miss Thornton has been on the phone and charmed you into speeding up our investigation."

"And I think she is right," Calderwood said eagerly, his hazel eyes sparkling. "We shouldn't waste time waiting for confirmation but strike while the trail is hot."

"An unfortunate turn of phrase," McCord remarked, "since the body is not even cold yet. Have you found anything to support Amy's theory?"

"I called the manager at Dine Murrayfield," Calderwood said, "and he confirmed that the family was there celebrating Mr Fisher's birthday at the time the fire broke out. But," he added before McCord could object, "he also said there was a right stooshie early on after which Victoria Norval left in a hurry. He wasn't in the room at the time but one of the staff told him. I said we'd come round to interview them later."

"Let's wait until we know who died in that fire, shall we? The family thinks it was a burglar, but they told me about the fallout at the party as well. Apparently, Victoria Norval threatened to reveal some terrible secret. But before you get too excited: the fire investigator told me the current main suspect is a cat. A dead cat, to be precise."

Calderwood's handsome face fell in disappointment, but he was not ready to give up yet. "At the very least, we've got a missing person inquiry, sir."

"As far as I know, nobody has reported Victoria Norval missing," McCord pointed out.

"Isn't that suspicious in itself?" Calderwood asked.

"Look," McCord said, "I know you are desperate to get stuck in after all that time in hospital, rehab and desk duty. But we still need to make sure we have a case before we go in all guns blazing. I need to give sound reasons to the Super for the allocation of resources, remember?"

As if he had heard his name mentioned across the corridor, Superintendent Arthur Gilchrist strode into the open-plan office and surveyed his kingdom. McCord groaned inwardly; he had hoped the boss would be spending his duty weekend hiding in the office, as usual.

"How is our hero today?" Gilchrist greeted Calderwood as he had done every time since the shooting three and a half months ago when Calderwood had thrown himself into the path of a bullet to save another man's life. Having survived an injury that would have killed a lesser man, he had then contracted a nasty infection that spread to his liver and delayed his recovery even more.

Calderwood blushed in embarrassment and ran a hand through his fair hair. "Perfectly well, sir, thank you."

"Excellent. And what have we here?" Gilchrist asked, perusing the board. "A new case you have failed to tell me about, DI McCord?"

McCord took a deep breath. Superintendent Gilchrist was a man of few talents, but he always managed to find something he could criticize McCord for. He seemed to have forgotten that McCord too had been injured during the same shooting incident and, alongside Calderwood, had been given a bravery award.

"A suspected murder case," McCord said with a side glance to Calderwood. "We are still waiting for final confirmation, but we have started preliminary inquiries. The fire where the victim was found happened on Ravelston Dykes Road" – McCord saw that the meaning of this address was not lost on Gilchrist, who was always anxious to please the upper classes of Edinburgh – "and we don't want to be seen as having been slow in our response, sir, do we?"

Gilchrist nodded. "No, indeed, we don't. Carry on, DI McCord, and report to me as soon as you have some new information."

Having given his troops the required support, he marched back to his office.

McCord grabbed a piece of paper, drew a cartoon sketch of a cat's face and wrote 'victim 2 / arsonist?' underneath.

Grinning at Calderwood, he pinned it on the board next to Victoria Norval's photo.

"Now let's wait and see if there actually has been a murder."

Chapter 3

At the start of a new working week, Amy Thornton was luxuriating in the morning sunshine streaming into the large windows of *Forth Write* magazine's premises in George Street, when her peace was shattered by raised voices coming out of the office of John Campbell, owner of the popular niche publication. John was every inch a gentleman and never quarrelled with his old university friend Martin Eden, current affairs editor and renowned cartoonist, although both men came from the opposite ends of the social and political spectrum.

Unless, that is, they argued about Amy who, apart from being responsible for fashion, human interest stories and the weekend supplement, was also the daughter of John's adored partner, Valerie. Both men had adopted Amy in their mind, if not in law, and competed fiercely for the position of chief protector. Amy loved them dearly but wished they would understand that she did not need any protection at all.

The office door was flung open, and Amy heard Martin shouting in his high-pitched voice, "You can't keep sending her abroad forever. A, it is both morally wrong and futile to keep her away from DI McCord, and B, the magazine can't afford all this air travel in the current climate."

"Why don't you tell Valerie that," John replied in his deep voice with its plummy upper-class accent. "She–"

Both men stepped into the main office and, seeing Amy sitting there glaring at them, stopped in their tracks.

"So, this is what was behind the magazine's sudden interest in European fashion houses," Amy said angrily. "Mum has been trying to keep me away from St Leonard's? And you are playing along with that, John? I never thought you could be so devious."

John looked hurt. "You must admit that you have been involved in dangerous situations, more than once, and last time you could easily have been killed! We were hoping that with a bit of distance, you might develop... different interests."

"Can I remind you that my interest in crime has dragged this magazine out of the red and made it a commercial success?"

"She is right, you know," Martin said.

For a moment, Amy was distracted by Martin's pink rhinestone suit that even by his standards was outrageous.

This was an opportunity Martin could not afford to miss.

"It is quite clear that Amy and DI McCord are destined for each other, and there is nothing anybody can do about it," he said to John, sure that his stance would win him the upper hand in the competition for Amy's affections, "and instead of putting obstacles in their way, we should be guiding them in the right direction."

Amy sighed. Martin loved playing Cupid, but he really did not have a clue what was going on. She raised her hands in despair.

"For the hundredth time, there is nothing going on between McCord and me, and I seriously doubt there ever will be. I just love playing detective. Maybe I should join the police force," she said, pretending to seriously consider this idea.

"Good Lord, no!" John exclaimed. "Your mother would never have a moment's peace, which means I would not have one either."

"Well, maybe you could tell her about my plans, which would make my collaboration with McCord seem the lesser of two evils?"

John regarded his protégée with the clear-eyed love of a father in every sense but the biological. "And you have the audacity to call *me* devious."

"Enough of the compliments," Amy said. "A body has been found in a burnt-out house on Ravelston Dykes Road, and it smells like murder to me. McCord is a bit slow on the uptake, as always, and I've got a lead already. So, no more fashion assignments, please, John, I'm going to be busy!"

* * *

Dr Cyril Crane, forensic pathologist with a short neck but a long list of letters after his name, was in a buoyant mood.

"Well done, DI McCord," he said, "I haven't had a burnt body for a while, and I don't want to get rusty."

"Let me make one thing clear, Dr Crane," McCord replied. "I did not set fire to this body in order to aid your professional development."

McCord always marvelled at the enjoyment Crane derived from examining dead bodies, a feeling McCord could not empathise with. Crane was fully aware of this and took sadistic pleasure in forcing McCord to view the remains as long as possible.

"Look here, DI McCord," Crane said, pointing to the charred corpse that had been carefully laid out on the examination table, "typical pugilistic posture: arms raised in defensive position, hand tightened into fists. What do you think this tells us?"

McCord averted his eyes from the burnt flesh and the shrunken skull and fastened them instead on the tuft of white hair that stood up cheerfully on the pathologist's head. He decided to humour Crane in the hope that he would prioritise this case over anybody else's.

"The victim was fighting off an attacker?"

Crane laughed heartily. "Quite the opposite, my dear chap. It indicates that the victim was alive but unconscious at the time of the fire."

"That means that the fire was not used to cover up a murder," McCord thought aloud.

"I can't see any blunt-force trauma or the like," Crane said, "but the victim could have been drugged, of course, which would explain why they did not try to escape."

"Several people claim that the wife was drunk less than an hour before the fire. Any chance of finding evidence of alcohol or drugs?" McCord asked. Judging by the shrivelled remains, this seemed impossible.

"Difficult after a fire," Crane said, "but I was able to extract some cells from the spinal cord and even a tiny bit of blood that might be sufficient for a toxicology report. The dental records should give you an ID as well, if all else fails. You'll have my report as soon as."

* * *

Once outside, McCord breathed in deeply. Although laced with the city centre car fumes, the air seemed fresh compared with the smell of death inside the mortuary. Even the depth of the usually dark and forbidding canyon that was Cowgate was illuminated by the warm rays of the sun, and there was a holiday atmosphere about the city that was infectious. McCord, in no rush to return to his stuffy office, pulled out his phone.

"Calderwood? What was the address of the Fishers' housekeeper again? Was she not staying with her sister somewhere in the city centre?"

"It was Niddry Street, I think," Calderwood said. "Hang on."

McCord heard Calderwood tapping on his computer.

"Yes, 48 Niddry Street."

"That's round the corner from here," McCord said, almost disappointed he did not have to walk further. "Thanks. I'll pay her a wee visit while I'm here. See you later at the station."

McCord walked on the pavement along the narrow, cobbled street past locked garages and graffitied walls until he found the entrance to the flat. As luck would have it, Miss Jennifer Hamill was at home. She was a woman in her early fifties, McCord guessed, but she looked as if she was not ready to succumb to middle age just yet. Her naturally brunette hair had been dyed professionally to hide the grey that was beginning to creep in, and dressed in loose, pale blue cotton trousers and a crisp white blouse, she still cut a fine figure. Her make-up was skilfully applied, but her eyes were heavy as if she had not slept much.

After examining McCord's ID, she readily invited him into the kitchen.

As he cautiously sat down on one of the wobbly chairs, she went about preparing them an iced drink with the speed and decisiveness of an efficient housekeeper.

"I wondered if somebody would come to speak to me. I've heard that a body was found in the house and that Ms Norval has gone missing. It wasn't her, was it?"

"We're still waiting for the results of the autopsy," McCord said. "But we're treating it as a suspicious death for now."

"Dear Lord," Jennifer Hamill said, prising some ice cubes out of a plastic tray. "I'm happy to help but I'm not sure how I can."

McCord took in the dirty skylight surrounded by mould where the rain had crept in, and the general shabbiness of the place only counteracted by the bunch of fresh flowers on the table.

"They came from Chloe, the Fishers' gardener," Jennifer Hamill said, noticing McCord's glance. "She dropped them off last night to cheer me up. You've met her?"

McCord nodded. "This must be quite a change for you from Roseburn House," he said, watching her pour cheap apple juice and soda into two glasses.

"You can say that again," Jennifer Hamill said. "But it is very good of my sister and her husband to take me in; they've fallen on hard times as you can see. The rents in Edinburgh are absolutely ridiculous. Seven hundred pounds a month they're paying for this..." – she refrained from using a more descriptive phrase – "flat. That's why I stayed at Roseburn House for so long. Rent-free living is quite a bonus."

"When did you start working for them?"

"It was when the first Mrs Fisher fell ill. I am a nurse by training and Mrs Fisher hated hospitals; she limited her visits there to days when her treatment made it necessary. For the rest of the time, I looked after her at home and helped around the house."

"Did the Fishers have a good marriage?"

Jennifer Hamill hesitated.

"Mr Fisher won't hear any of this," McCord reassured her. "I'm only gathering background information."

"On the face of it, they got on well. There were no arguments that I heard, and Mrs Fisher never complained. She was the good, old-fashioned sort, you know, a homemaker, supportive of her husband, no matter what he did."

She did not elaborate on what Fisher might have done.

"Victoria Norval is quite different, I guess?" McCord asked.

"Oh, yes. She is much younger, very independent, very... modern. Mr Fisher fell head over heels for her even before his wife had passed away. He didn't say anything, of course, but I could tell by the way he was pulling in his stomach and splashing aftershave about, and always humming he was. I hope that Mrs Fisher never cottoned on, but she was very frail by that time and the medication made her very sleepy. After her death, Mr Fisher asked if I would stay on as a housekeeper, and considering what nurses are paid these days and the working conditions in hospitals, I had quite a good deal there. Mr Fisher and Ms Norval got married a year after Mrs Fisher's death. There was a bit of an uproar when she decided to keep her own name, but she stuck to her guns."

"Do you know of any secret that Ms Norval might have wanted to reveal?"

"A secret?" Jennifer Hamill looked puzzled. "About what?"

"Mr Fisher? Maybe something to do with his business? Or a private matter?"

Jennifer Hamill shook her head. "I have no idea, sorry."

"What is Victoria Norval like as a person?" McCord asked.

"I didn't see much of her, really; she was very busy with her career, and Mr Fisher soon tired of her being away doing her own thing rather than seeing to his needs, as he put it. There were a lot of arguments. But she was always nice to me, I have to say. She was also very good to Chloe who's a lovely girl, very hard-working," Jennifer Hamill continued. "She saw to the garden and did some of this rewilding that is all the rage now. Though, if you ask me, all it did was make an awful mess of the back garden."

"And how does Ms Norval get on with Mr Fisher's children?" McCord asked.

"She tried quite hard at the beginning, but they didn't make it easy for her. I think they resented her coming into their father's life, especially Danielle, the daughter – she adores her father. Sometimes children are jealous of their parents' new partners, maybe that's why she hardly ever visited. Shame, really, Mr Fisher rarely got to see his grandson. He is something else, is Hunter."

"I know, I've met him," McCord said with a grin. "What about Patrick, the son?"

"He was living at home, of course, and I suspect when Ms Norval came onto the scene, he was worried about his inheritance. And then there was the big falling-out a couple of weeks ago–"

Jennifer Hamill stopped herself, but it was too late.

"A falling-out? About what?" McCord asked.

"Ms Norval felt that it was time that Patrick found himself a job. 'All you ever do is sit around not writing your second novel,' she told him, and next thing, Mr Fisher announces that he agrees with her – that was a novelty, I can tell you – and that Patrick had until the end of the month to get his life in order before his allowance was cut. Patrick was furious and called his stepmother a gold-digger. Happy families, eh?"

She took a sip from her drink.

"Now, Saturday, the day of the fire," McCord said. "Can you tell me what happened?"

"I really don't know anything about it," Jennifer Hamill said. "Mr Fisher had given me the evening off because they were all going out to celebrate his birthday. I went to the Playhouse with a friend to see *The Phantom of the Opera*, so I left the house at six. The show finished around nine thirty, which was when I switched my phone back on and saw Chloe's missed calls and texts about the fire. I could not believe it; I had to go and see it for myself. By the time I arrived around ten, the family had decamped to The Braemar. I went round there to see if I could help in any way, but Mr Fisher was very short with me and told me to leave them in peace. I suppose they were all in shock."

McCord, picturing the scene, thought that a very generous interpretation on the housekeeper's part. "What did you do then? You had lost *your* home as well."

"I slept on Chloe's sofa that night, and yesterday, I moved in here. I realise that I might have to find another job, but I keep hoping Mr Fisher will call to tell me what he plans to do for the future. Naturally, they don't really need me now that they are staying at The Braemar, but surely, they won't be there for much longer. And I'll need paying by the end of the month!"

She pointed to her pristine outfit.

"I had to buy new clothes and everything. I hope the insurance will cover that as well. And all my personal papers, bank statements, letters; all gone! It's such a nightmare!"

Her face contorted slightly, and she closed her eyes.

Keen to distract her from her troubles and avoid being alone with a crying female, McCord swiftly moved on with his questioning.

"The fire investigator told me that it is likely that the fire started in the living room around an ashtray that was knocked down on the floor by a cat that had come in through an open window."

Jennifer Hamill frowned. "That can't be right. The only smoker in the family is Mr Fisher, and he is very careful about putting out his cigars. He used to own an insurance company, you know."

"I know, yes," McCord said. "So everybody keeps telling me."

"That's how he made his money, I believe," Jennifer Hamill said. "I've always said that the premiums we pay are far too high. Anyway, he would never leave a burning cigar lying around. And," she continued most emphatically, "I remember distinctly closing all the windows before I left, which was not long before they all went to the party. So, your story of how the fire started doesn't make any sense!"

No, it doesn't, and how I hate it when it doesn't, McCord thought.

* * *

That Monday afternoon, as McCord entered St Leonard's, he was wondering if he should set the awesome machine that was Edinburgh CID in motion or wait until the fire investigation officer had found definite proof of arson.

His inner debate was interrupted by DS Walter Struthers who had shed his obligatory cardigan and sported only a white shirt whose buttons struggled to fasten across his expanding stomach. Everybody has their cross to bear, and McCord's consisted of Superintendent Gilchrist, who represented the long, vertical beam of the cross, and Struthers, who was the shorter, horizontal one. For reasons nobody could fathom, Gilchrist had promoted the racist and misogynistic Struthers to the position of detective sergeant, and it was a constant struggle for McCord to find the incompetent, lazy officer something to do that he could not mess up. McCord had gone to great lengths to get rid of him during the last investigation but cruel twists of fate, mainly in the shape of Gilchrist, had thrown the DS back into his path.

With a self-satisfied smile, Struthers placed a file on McCord's desk. "The witness statement you asked for."

"What witness?" McCord asked.

"Chloe Chalmers, the gardener at Roseburn House. She came in this morning while you were at the morgue. Pretty girl."

McCord wasn't sure what annoyed him more; the fact that he had missed Chalmers's visit, or the way Struthers talked about her.

He flicked open the file.

"And what did she say?"

"She has no idea who or what might have caused the fire. She went for a walk round the nearby golf course, and when she returned, the house was on fire. She spoke to one of the neighbours on her way, who can confirm the times, she says."

"Good," McCord said. "Did you ask her about the family and if she noticed anything unusual around the time of the fire?"

"Should I have?" Struthers asked, perplexed.

McCord drew in a sharp breath and expelled the air in a little explosion. "That is what one normally asks a witness, DS Struthers. But never mind."

Struthers had waddled off when Jack Carruthers, the duty sergeant, called to say that someone with important information regarding the arson case was downstairs and asking to see him. McCord noticed that the way Carruthers spoke sounded strangely compressed, but he put it down to a cold and asked him to send the visitor up.

When five minutes later nobody had appeared, McCord left his desk and walked along the corridor to the large open-plan office. There, he found Calderwood giving an autograph to a delighted Hunter.

"What is going on?" McCord asked. "Why is this child roaming around the station?"

He turned to Hunter. "You're not here on your own, are you? Where is your mother?"

Hunter looked offended. "At the hotel, in the spa suite. I am quite capable of taking a taxi to St Leonard's police station on my own, you know. I'm not a baby!"

McCord saw the grinning faces of the officers that had gathered round the boy.

"Okay, okay," he said soothingly. "Let's hear it then. What important information do you have relating to the fire?"

Pleased at finally being taken seriously, Hunter pulled himself up to his full height.

"I am sure that the cat did not cause the fire," he said.

"Aha," McCord said, "and why not?"

"Because" – Hunter paused for effect – "that was Hamish, the neighbours' cat. He disappeared the day before the fire. Hamish was very old – eighteen, I think – and he was also sick and could hardly walk anymore, so there is no way he could have jumped up onto the windowsill and then onto a table knocking down the ashtray."

He held up a clear, zipped-up freezer bag containing short, black strands of hair. "Here, I got those from the neighbours so that you can compare the DNA."

McCord took the proffered bag, momentarily lost for words. The smirks of the gathered team had morphed into open-mouthed astonishment.

"But how did the cat get into the house if he couldn't get in through the window?" asked Calderwood.

Hunter, having had the advantage of a day's thinking about the mystery of the dead cat, was ready with an explanation.

"I think the person who burnt the house down must have come across Hamish's dead body and decided to frame him for the arson. Then he must have put Hamish on the floor, with the ashtray next to him, and opened the window to make everyone believe Hamish had come in that way and caused the fire."

Hunter's obvious delight at his deductive prowess, however, soon gave way to grave concern. "I do hope Hamish was already dead before that. If he wasn't, you are not looking for an ordinary killer but a dangerous psychopath."

McCord could not help but be impressed with the boy's cognitive abilities although his moral priorities still needed some development.

He formally shook Hunter's hand.

"DS Calderwood, please take this young detective to the canteen for a hot chocolate and a muffin and then put him in a taxi back to The Braemar."

Calderwood led a beaming Hunter towards the exit, while the other officers were left standing there, staring after the boy.

"What are you lot waiting for?" McCord said. "We have a murder investigation to run!"

Chapter 4

Amy got up from her desk chair, moved to the window and gazed down George Street to give her tired eyes a rest from the computer screen. The sunny spell continued, and some of the stern, grey façades opposite shone golden in the late morning light. Cars drove past with their windows open and music blaring out of them in waves of cheerful noise; pedestrians, normally wrapped in warm jackets with turned-up collars, were sporting shorts, miniskirts, and sleeveless tops. Pale or sunburnt flesh was being exposed in abundance. Amy thought of the tanned elegance of the people in Paris and Milan and, for purely aesthetic reasons, almost wished Edinburgh's cold easterly back.

She had been working flat out most of the previous day on her theory about who had killed Victoria Norval. McCord, who seemed obsessed with finding scientific proof, might still be holding back, but she had no doubts that the body was hers.

After spending several hours scouring social media, she still had not found what she was desperate to know: the identity of the man featured in Victoria Norval's last Twitter post. Most of them were inconsequential at best, but this, Amy thought, could well lead her to Norval's killer.

The photograph was a selfie that showed Norval's smiling face and the back of the head, neck and shoulders of a man. By the looks of it, they were dancing, holding each other close. She was winking into the camera, sharing the amusement about the secretly taken picture with the viewer.

The caption underneath read, 'Finally found happiness! No more hiding!' She had added no fewer than five smileys.

Convinced that Norval's intention of revealing the identity of her secret lover played a part in her death, Amy went back to her desk and sifted through a couple more months on Norval's Twitter feed but could not detect this man. No wonder: apart from neatly cut brown hair above a long, slim neck there was nothing to be seen of him. Also, being married to Morton Fisher, Norval had probably been very careful about keeping the affair secret.

Amy's search was interrupted by the sound of a key turning in the door, and then her mother breezed into the room. Valerie Thornton was pushing fifty but looked nothing like it. She looked nothing like Amy either. Dressed in a Greek-style dress that showed off her height and stunning curves, she had pinned up her long, auburn hair that was sufficiently dishevelled to be endearing. Displaying a cheerful indifference to what people might think of her, she had the charisma of a film star. No wonder John had fallen head over heels in love with her. And, on balance, Amy had to admit, Valerie had been an amazing mum, bringing her up on her own in humble circumstances, full of love for her girl and equally full of distrust towards all men, in particular the men who might ruin Amy's life. Since then, John had been the only lover with whom she had had a relationship, and Amy was delighted that Valerie had found someone on whom she could bestow at least some of that overwhelming love.

Valerie rushed towards Amy and gave her that special hug that always threatened to break a rib or two.

"Hi, sweetie," Valerie said. "I haven't seen you all week. That flaming deadline for the winter collection is driving me crazy. Who wants to think about winter clothes in this weather?"

She flapped her arms in a comical gesture of attempting to cool herself down. "Is John in? I need to speak to him about Le Nuage. They want me to come to Paris for their show, but I won't go unless John comes as well. You can't trust those Frenchmen." She winked at her daughter. Amy's father had been a language teacher from Paris who had abandoned Valerie when she was pregnant.

Although it was six months ago that Amy and Valerie had ritually destroyed all the letters that Amy had written to her absent father and never sent, the fact that she had never met her father still stung Amy. She had not even told her mum that every so often she studied the one picture that existed of him, always wondering what he was like. But she knew in her heart that this was not a discussion that Valerie wanted to have ever again.

"John's out," Amy said. "He's in some meeting."

"That explains why he is not answering his phone," Valerie said. "What are you working on?"

"I've been busy trying to find a guy on social media for an article of mine," Amy said.

Well, it wasn't a lie.

"Why is he difficult to find? Don't you know his name?"

"No. He was the lover of a married woman, and they were very discreet. I haven't even seen his face before," Amy added. "I only have a picture of the back of his head and neck."

"That's not much," Valerie said. "Can I see?"

Amy put Norval's selfie on the screen. Valerie peered at it closely.

"Can you zoom in a bit? On the bottom part?"

"What for?" Amy asked. "Did I miss a mole or something?"

"No," Valerie sad impatiently. "I'd thought with your background you'd be more switched on. Look!" She pointed to the collar of his suit. "That cloth," she said dreamily, "the delicate dark stripe, barely visible. And the stitching. You don't get that from a sweatshop in Bangladesh."

"So, you're saying that is a very expensive suit," Amy said. "And how does that help?"

"There won't be many like it in Edinburgh," Valerie said. "He'll have worn it on other formal occasions. Look for the suit, not the man."

Amy blew her a kiss.

"You are a genius, Mum. And unless they met on a dating site, she'll have met him at one of her friends' or clients' parties. I'll check her closest contacts first."

She started typing excitedly.

"Hang on," Valerie said, suddenly alarmed. "For what kind of article would you need to find a man who's trying hard to remain anonymous? You're not chasing deranged killers again with DI McCord, are you? I thought that was all finished!"

Amy swivelled around in her chair and pointed an accusing finger at her mother.

"And you did your best to achieve that, didn't you? Manipulating John to send me all around Europe to keep me away from St Leonard's! That was completely out of line!"

Valerie was unrepentant.

"Don't point your finger at me, girl. How many times have I told you, it's rude? Anyway, what was I supposed to do? You wouldn't see sense, and when that madman almost killed you–"

"He didn't–" Amy attempted to make her point, but in vain.

"You're right," Valerie shouted, "not he, they! Four times, *four times*, your life has been in jeopardy because DI McCord allowed you to tag along on his investigations. Utterly irresponsible, I say."

"Don't blame McCord. It's not his fault!" Amy said heatedly. "*I* wanted to be part of those investigations. God knows, he never gave me the slightest encouragement; on the contrary!"

"Isn't he in charge? He's the one who is supposed to be the investigating officer, not you! It's his job to get shot, not yours!"

"Mum," Amy said urgently, grabbing Valerie's hot hands, "Mum, this is what I want to do. It's what I need to do. I realised that when I was in Paris and Milan and all these other places; all I wanted was to come back and help McCord crack a case. That's what makes me happy. You want me to be happy, don't you?"

"Of course, I do," Valerie said, tears in her eyes now. "But I also need to know that you are safe. I couldn't bear it if anything happened to you."

Amy stepped forward and gave her mum a rib crunching hug. "You don't need to worry. DI McCord and Calderwood will make sure that nothing happens to me."

Valerie sighed. "That's what Martin always says. According to him, DI McCord is Edinburgh's answer to James Bond as well as your destiny. But then, that's Martin we're talking about."

Amy laughed.

"I know he is prone to exaggeration, and he has completely the wrong idea about me and McCord, but Martin is right about what matters: McCord is smart and brave, and nothing is going to happen to me when we are together. In fact, I'm much safer when I am with him than when I'm investigating on my own, so you should be glad, really."

Here, Valerie's abating agitation flared up again.

"I should be glad? Are you kidding me?"

Quite serious now, Amy grabbed her mother by the upper arms and shook her.

"Glad or not, you have to accept this situation. I'm not a child anymore, I'm a grown woman. You've lived your life the way you chose to, and so will I – either with your blessing or without. But I'd much rather have it."

Valerie collapsed on a chair. "I don't want to lose you, my girl," she whispered.

Amy bent down and gave her a smacker of a kiss on the cheek.

"You won't, Mum, I promise."

Eventually, Valerie retreated upstairs to the flat she shared with John to fix her make-up and fortify herself with a gin and tonic, and Amy was able to return to her investigation.

Her mum was right. It was likely that Norval had met this man through one of her acquaintances, so she made a list of those featured most often in her posts and went through their social media accounts. After countless selfies of people looking ecstatic for no particular reason, advice on how to cook twenty eggs at once in case all your friends stay over for breakfast, and photos of cats playing the piano, she finally came across a series of pictures from a wedding where among the dancing couples she found Norval and a tall, rather handsome man with brown hair and a long neck. He wore a stunning suit, and as Amy zoomed in, she saw the familiar pattern and delicate stitching. The man was tagged as James Palmer-Wycliffe.

Gotcha, Amy thought. Now, let's see what your story is.

Chapter 5

Crane was as good as his word and sent the post-mortem results less than twenty-four hours after McCord's visit at the morgue. Both DNA analysis and dental records showed that the body at Roseburn House was indeed that of Victoria Norval. McCord was relieved not to have made a fool of himself in front of Gilchrist, but at the same time, he was annoyed that Amy had been proved right, at least as far as the identity of the victim was concerned.

Norval had considerable amounts of alcohol and tranquillisers in her blood, but, as Crane had already indicated, the post-mortem showed no cause of death other than asphyxiation by toxic smoke.

"That means that somebody knew she was alone in the house, drunk and sleepy, and took the opportunity to set the house on fire to kill her, hoping it would look like an accident," Calderwood said.

McCord nodded. "And who is always the first point of call in a murder inquiry? The spouse."

With due caution, McCord approached the workstation of DC Sutton, nicknamed Heather the Hacker by colleagues who were frightened and in awe of her in equal measures. Her exceptional love of data was only surpassed by her loathing of humans. McCord was a notable exception because he respected her needs and behaved towards her not like a boss but like a grateful recipient of the information she extracted from the darkest corners of the web.

It had been Superintendent Gilchrist, who, under the pretence of inclusivity but in truth out of spite, had landed his obstreperous DI with a woman so far on the spectrum that she had once hacked into the police commissioner's bank accounts based on a metaphorical instruction she had taken literally. This transgression, which she in her childlike innocence had afterwards openly admitted, almost ended her career. Although she was still unsure how it had all come about, she did understand that this post with St Leonard's CID was her last-chance saloon and that it was essential to keep her mouth shut.

McCord, contrary to Gilchrist's intentions, had come to value this colleague who completed any given task without burdening him with the question of whether the methods she employed were legal or not.

She had assured him before in very few words that if they should be in the latter category, she would never be caught again.

In return, DC Sutton enjoyed a few privileges; she rarely had to deal with anybody apart from McCord and she had his permission to surround her desk with several layers of defensive structures that sheltered her from the outside world.

McCord gently knocked on the outer layer, consisting of obsolete filing cabinets, and after hearing a croaky 'come in', proceeded to the centre.

DC Sutton turned her long, horsey head to face McCord but her eyes, hugely enlarged by blue-tinted glasses, did not meet his; they fastened on a button halfway down his favourite maroon shirt.

Greetings were deemed to be an unnecessary convention by both of them; as always, McCord came straight to the point.

"Morton Fisher of Ravelston Dykes Road. I need to know anything that he might want to keep secret. Illegal business dealings, sex with minors, murder of his first wife, cruelty to animals, anything at all. He will have realised by now that he is a suspect in Victoria Norval's murder, so he might try to cover his, eh" – McCord remembered not to use any metaphorical language – "to hide any criminal activity by destroying files, etc."

A little smile played around DC Sutton's mouth as if to say, let him try. Without a word, she turned her eyes back to the screen and started caressing the keys at mind-boggling speed. Thus, the meeting had concluded successfully, and McCord quietly withdrew.

Outside DC Sutton's fortress, Calderwood was bouncing on his heels, bursting to pass on the latest good news.

"Sir, Bill Reid, the fire investigator, has been in touch and emailed the full report. They have confirmed that the fire started in the main living room around the ashtray, but he also said that the batteries in the smoke alarms were missing."

"Another indication that we are dealing with a premeditated killing," McCord said. "Anything else?"

"They found Norval's mobile phone."

"Surely, that is no use after being in the fire?" McCord asked.

"That's what I thought too, but the phone was on the bedroom floor, and, apparently, the temperature at floor level can be around a hundred degrees during a fire, which is much lower than the few hundred degrees at eye level. Reid said there was a good chance that forensics would be able to retrieve at least some data from the SIM card."

McCord punched the air in delight. "Great. I bet we'll find some interesting messages. The killer probably thought that the phone would be destroyed in the fire. Anything new on Fisher?"

"He used to own an insurance company but sold it ten years ago," Calderwood said. "Must have made a tidy sum to be able to afford Roseburn House. Now he runs a string of betting shops. Nothing illegal so far."

"I've already put Sutton onto him; if there's anything to find, she'll find it."

They made their way back to McCord's office, which was known among colleagues as 'Sunset Boulevard'. McCord, somewhat by mistake, had it painted burnt sienna during the last spate of renovations. He was used to the vibrant colour by now, but even if he had hated it, the fact that Superintendent Gilchrist's face contorted in pain any time he ventured into McCord's office, fully justified his choice.

When McCord opened the door, his heart skipped a beat.

In the visitor's chair, as if it were hers by right, sat Amy, her slim legs crossed under a pastel blue linen suit that contrasted beautifully with her olive skin and dark hair. Seeing the two men, she rose in a fluid, elegant move.

"Superintendent Gilchrist told me to come straight in," she said. "Judging by the way he was fawning over me, he must have sorely missed my articles extolling the excellence of Edinburgh CID and its senior leaders."

There was an awkward moment when Amy came towards them, and McCord was unsure whether to shake her hand or not.

"Do you have something for us, Miss Thornton, or have you come yet again to pump us for information?" he asked with the snarky tone they always employed with each other.

"A bit of both, McCord. How are you, Duncan?" she asked solicitously.

Calderwood, less inhibited and much more socially adept, kissed Amy lightly on the cheek, obviously delighted to see her.

"I'm fine," he said, smiling. "Can everybody please stop asking after my health as if I'm still in a critical condition? It's been a long time coming, but I'm as good as new."

"Wonderful!" Amy said, sitting down again. "I've been so worried about you!"

"Then you should have stayed here instead of faffing around with ridiculous clothes all over Europe," McCord said, but his jocular tone had an edge to it. "Do you know what it was like being stuck here on my own with Struthers? If it hadn't been for Turner and Dharwan, I might have jumped off the Forth Road Bridge."

Amy laughed but her mirth was tinged with guilt. It was only now she realised how much McCord must have missed Calderwood, and maybe even her. It was good to know that eager PC Mike Turner and loyal PC Surina Dharwan had been around to watch McCord's back. But now the team was finally together again to solve a murder.

"Anything interesting come up yet?" Amy asked. "I know you usually lag behind, but I wondered…"

"The reason things are moving slowly is that we are doing them professionally," McCord retorted. "We are gathering evidence, not gossip like certain people."

Amy threw back her head, exhaling loudly.

"Isn't it funny, though, how the gossip of certain people invariably leads you to the killer in the end. Or has the shock of being shot caused you memory loss?"

McCord shrugged. Having established their respective roles and with the ritual of mutual accusations out of the way, they could get down to business.

"It looks like the fire was started deliberately–"

"Which is what I told you from the beginning–"

"And at the moment, we have the husband, Morton Fisher, in the frame as our main suspect. At the party just before the fire, Victoria Norval told him in front of all the other guests that she was leaving him and threatened some sort of exposé."

"Doesn't he have an alibi if he was at the party?" Amy asked.

"I interviewed the staff at the restaurant," Calderwood said, "and they told me that because it was a buffet rather than a sit-down meal and because it was a hot day, the guests were milling around outside a lot of the time. But several people noticed that after Victoria's outburst, Fisher disappeared and was not seen for a while."

"Which would be quite natural after being humiliated in front of everybody," Amy interjected.

"Thing is," Calderwood continued, "nobody is sure how long he was away. It takes no more than about ten minutes to walk from the restaurant to the house. The killer could have sneaked out and been back within half an hour, but Fisher was definitely at the restaurant when the family were told about the fire at Roseburn, and then all of them returned home."

"We've also got Norval's phone that might give us a clue about what she was up to that evening," McCord said. "The other family members have told us she went off to see her boyfriend, but they could be lying, of course. Unfortunately, we don't know who he is; Norval seems to have kept it a secret from everybody. We've asked the housekeeper, but she doesn't know, and usually, they know everything."

"See, this is where yours truly comes in," Amy said. "Rather than gossiping, I have been doing research on the Internet and I have found Norval's mystery lover. James Palmer-Wycliffe."

She put a printout from his website on the desk.

"He sounds posh," McCord said. "I hate him already."

Amy laughed. "Born and bred in Morningside like most great people," she said with a wink to Calderwood who hailed from the same area, "educated at Fettes, degree from LSE. Runs a consultancy firm, which isn't doing great. But this is why you should have a look at him."

With a flourish, she placed a copy of Norval's last tweet on top of the other photograph. "It seems Norval was on a mission to expose the men around her," Amy said.

"How on earth did you identify him from that?" Calderwood asked.

"Through the collar of his suit. With a little help from my mum," she admitted.

McCord scanned the picture and the caption of the Twitter post. "Amy, I know you must have spent ages on it, but I don't think this is getting us much further. The whole family suspected she was having an affair anyway. She told them as much at the party. That was not the secret she was threatening to reveal. Besides, having met Fisher, I doubt he would kill his wife over an affair. There didn't seem to be much love lost between them."

"Still," Calderwood pointed out, "no man likes being cuckolded in public, no matter how bad the marriage was. It's not about love, it's about pride."

Amy was getting increasingly frustrated.

"Surely, in a murder inquiry, you'd be interested in the victim's extra-marital affairs? But you're missing the point. Both Norval and Palmer-Wycliffe were very careful not to reveal the affair up to that point. The photo suggests that Palmer-Wycliffe didn't realise he was being photographed. What if he wanted to keep the affair secret for his own reasons?"

"That may well be true," McCord said, "but I don't think that all this helps us nail Fisher. Still, it's good to have confirmation that she was having an affair, and it would be useful to know what exactly was going on between Norval and this – what's his name?"

"Palmer-Wycliffe," Amy said through gritted teeth.

"Exactly. Why don't you follow this up, Amy, while we concentrate on Fisher?"

Amy shot up, nostrils flaring.

"In other words, you investigate who you think is the real suspect, while I can keep myself amused with what you see as my outlandish theories! Patronising or what! Well, let's see who's first to come up with something useful, shall we?"

She snatched the photographs of Palmer-Wycliffe from McCord's desk and marched out of the office, leaving behind a bewildered McCord who looked at Calderwood for support but was only given an incredulous shake of the head in return.

Chapter 6

Amy thought it was unlikely that James Palmer-Wycliffe would pour his heart out to a journalist when confronted with his lover's post, so she decided to delay her attack until she had found out more about him.

In order to be able to work on the case in an unofficial manner, she had persuaded John to let her write an obituary on Victoria Norval, which would necessitate, of course, an interview with her family.

There had been very little enthusiasm on the family's part, but they could hardly say no when asked to pay tribute to their wife and stepmother who had met such a terrible end.

As it was another glorious, very hot day without even the slightest breeze, Morton Fisher and his children graciously received Amy on one of the secluded patios at The Braemar. After a waiter had provided them with cool drinks and snacks, the family reeled off their statements, which, it seemed to Amy, had been prepared in advance.

Fisher professed to be devastated by his beautiful wife's death. According to him, she had been 'adventurous' and 'full of life'. Amy wondered if that was a euphemism for her affair with Palmer-Wycliffe. Fisher was obviously assuming that the police would not share details of their conversation with the press and hoping that the few witnesses to his deceased wife's accusations would be discreet or at least not widely quoted. When he had finished talking about his late wife, he folded his fleshy arms across his chest. There was nothing else to be had from him, Amy decided, so she turned to Patrick Fisher.

"And what about you, Mr Fisher, what do you want to tell the readers of *Forth Write* magazine?"

Patrick Fisher crossed his legs in a studied pose of relaxation.

"Do call me Patrick, please," he said with a charming smile. "Victoria was a wonderful woman, and I was so pleased for Dad to have found happiness again after Mum died."

"You must have got on well if you were still living at home," Amy remarked.

Patrick Fisher's smile became a little strained. "Family is the most important thing, isn't it? And you know what the rents are like in Edinburgh. As an aspiring author, they are beyond my means, and there was plenty of room in the house. Why go elsewhere when the people you love are right here?"

His father choked on his IPA but recovered his countenance quickly.

Danielle McLellan was the most nervous of the three, maybe because she was the least accustomed to lying. Amy wondered if it was the heat or anxiety which made her sweat so profusely that her short, flared cotton skirt was sticking to her thighs. As she flipped it up, Amy noticed several small round scars on her inner thighs and bruises that, judging by their fading black and yellow hues, were about a week old. Aware of Amy's glance, Danielle McLellan hastily pulled the skirt down as much as it would go and kept her legs firmly clamped together for the rest of the interview.

"And what would you say your stepmother's legacy is?" Amy asked her.

"I greatly admired her drive and business sense. Did you know she built up her company from nothing? She was an inspiration to young women in Scotland."

Danielle McLellan seemed to have lost the thread of her speech. She tugged at her long sleeves as if she too needed to find some inspiration.

"Of course, she was a wonderful person, too. Daddy simply adored her and spoiled her rotten." Sensing that this could be misconstrued, she hastily continued. "He is just a very generous man."

Amy saw the adoration in her face and gently inquired how long she had been staying with her father and Victoria.

"Hunter and I only arrived the day before the fire. It was awful. Poor Daddy."

She reached across the small table to squeeze her father's hand, who patted her arm patronisingly with the other.

Rather exhausted from the deluge of clichés she had taken down in her notebook, Amy decided to liven things up a bit.

With an apologetic smile, she pulled out the photograph of James Palmer-Wycliffe.

"Do any of you happen to recognise this man?" she asked, looking at the three family members in turn.

"Why should we?" Morton Fisher's voice now had an aggressive undertone.

"He has been linked to your wife," Amy said innocently, "most likely malicious rumours, of course. I was wondering if any of you saw him around the time of the fire?"

"You think it was him who set fire to my house?" he asked, his eyes narrowed.

"There is nothing to suggest that," Amy said blandly.

"Do you know who he is?"

"I'd rather not say, I may well be wrong."

Danielle McLellan picked up the photo and then passed it on to her brother.

"I didn't see him around, but I was too distraught to notice anything."

Patrick Fisher briefly shrugged and handed Palmer-Wycliffe's picture back to Amy.

"I hope you're not going to print any of these rumours?" Morton Fisher said.

"I always make sure that everything in my articles is the truth," Amy said, thinking of the times she had praised Superintendent Gilchrist's leadership qualities. Well, there was a price to pay for being allowed into the inner sanctum of Edinburgh CID.

"Never mind, I think I have lovely quotes to get on with," Amy said and rose from her chair. "Thank you all very much, and again, you have my deepest condolences. I am getting the feeling that Victoria was a very special person."

There was the briefest of pauses, then Morton Fisher said what was expected. "She was. I take it you will send me a draft of what you write before it is published. I'm looking forward to reading your article. Goodbye."

Sometimes anticipation is better than the event, Amy thought, hoping she would not be reduced to putting her name under this drivel.

As she turned to go, she suddenly had an idea. Since she was in the area anyway, she would see if somebody else was around who might tell her more about the oh-so-happy Fisher family.

* * *

Amy was in luck. The driveway into Roseburn House was still cordoned off, but no officer of the law was to be seen. Amy ducked under the tape and walked up to the house that lay there hollowed out and abandoned. At the back of the garden, Amy found the young woman she had rushed past the day after the fire. She was watering some flowerpots, ably assisted by a little boy who regarded Amy with uninhibited curiosity.

"Who are you?" he asked her.

"I'm Amy Thornton. I work for *Forth Write* magazine."

"I'm Hunter McLellan. I'm helping Chloe this afternoon."

Amy smiled. She had hoped to come across Morton Fisher's grandson during the interview and had wondered where he was.

"Very pleased to meet you, Hunter. I was speaking to your mum, uncle, and granddad only a few minutes ago."

Hunter's smile faded. "Oh no. Were they looking for me?"

"Why, don't they know you're here?" Amy asked, now concerned herself.

"They wouldn't have let me come," he said by means of an explanation, "and I like being here with Chloe."

The young woman smiled. "Hi. I'm Chloe Chalmers, the gardener. Hunter's quite safe with me, and I'll walk him to the hotel afterwards."

"Were you here during the fire by any chance?" Amy asked.

"Not really. I was out for a walk when it happened. I had a chat with old Mr Haynes when I passed his house. I spoke to him twice in fact. First, on my way to the golf course and again when I came back. He is quite lonely, poor soul, and tends to witter on a bit, so I came home later than I had planned..." Chalmers was welling up. "If I had come straight home, maybe I could have called the fire brigade earlier and prevented the fire from spreading, and Ms Norval..." She pulled a hankie from her pocket and wiped her tears away. "Why are you asking?"

Amy pulled the picture of James Palmer-Wycliffe from her bag. "Did you see this man hanging around the house before or after the fire? Or in the days leading up to it?"

Chalmers studied the man's features. "Yes. I did, actually. He was standing at the gate with the other onlookers when I came back from my walk. I was desperate to see what was going on and wanted to know if my cottage was on fire as well. I noticed him because I had to ask him to move aside to let me through. He seemed quite mesmerised by the fire."

Amy was scribbling furiously in her notebook. "Do you know if he had any connection to the family?"

"I think he could be Victoria's boyfriend," Hunter butted in. "When we got back to the house and saw it was on fire, I asked Uncle Patrick where she was, and he said that she had gone off with a man and probably set the house on fire as she went."

"Really," Amy said. "Do you know anything else about this man, by any chance?"

Hunter shook his head regretfully. "Mum and I arrived the day before the fire, and we aren't here all that often. Normally, Victoria would have chatted with me – she liked me, you see – but this time she was in a very bad mood. I'm sure she had been crying and she hardly spoke to me at all. And the next morning, when Grandpa was away golfing, she was in his study for a long time, searching for something in his desk drawers. When she saw me, she looked guilty and told me to go away. I went but I stuck my head round the door again and saw her sneaking a notebook or something into her pocket. It must have been important."

"That's very interesting. Did your mum and uncle get on well with Victoria?" Amy asked.

"They pretended to when Mum and I arrived, but in the evening, I couldn't sleep, so I crept downstairs again and heard Uncle Patrick say that Victoria was only after Grandpa's money, and Mum said that Grandpa had been a fool to marry her. I remember that because normally they don't agree on anything."

Amy looked at Chalmers who smiled through her tears in confirmation.

"She was really nice, actually," Chalmers said. "I had the impression that she was passionate about her business and disappointed in Mr Fisher because he didn't take it very seriously. The one time he was out here, he argued with her. 'It's a nice little job you've got there,' he told her. 'But the real money is elsewhere'."

"And what did Ms Norval say to that?" Amy asked.

"She was furious and said money wasn't everything. She was also the only one who was interested in the rewilding project. It was her who employed me, you see. Mr Fisher never even checked up on me. He was pleased, though, when I told him that in a couple of years' time, they would hardly need to do any gardening at all in this area."

"Would you mind showing me around the garden?" Amy asked. "It would be nice to include the rewilding project in the obituary I've been asked to write, as part of her legacy, as it were."

"Of course. No problem," Chalmers said. "I'm sure it'll be okay if you take some pictures."

"Great," Amy said. "The place is glorious in the sunshine."

Hunter, not overly excited at the prospect of a tour of the garden, nudged Amy's arm. "Do you think I should tell the police about that notebook Victoria took?"

Amy smiled. "You're quite the little detective, aren't you? If you like, I can let DI McCord know."

"Are you his girlfriend?" Hunter asked.

Amy felt herself blush. "No, I'm not. But I know him quite well."

Hunter thought about this for a moment. "I think I'd rather tell him myself. Adults always forget. But thanks, anyway."

Chapter 7

Driving towards his childhood home in Niddrie, a poor part of Edinburgh languishing to the south-east of the city centre, McCord was contemplating the topic of families.

There were the Fishers of this world, rolling in money, enjoying the benefits of a private education and every luxury, and yet, there was no love he could detect, only blatant self-interest. The father was jealously guarding his money, while the children were eyeing up the inheritance. McCord's start in life could not have been more different. Growing up in a deprived area had not been easy. Meeting Morton Fisher, however, had reminded him how lucky he was to have Keith McCord as his father.

The evening sun had turned the rusty iron railings into brass and the cracked flagstones into gold when McCord walked towards the entrance of the dilapidated building. His father still lived in the same council flat he had been allocated when he first got married to McCord's mother.

They did not know then that she had only eleven months left to live. Shielded by blissful ignorance, they had been jubilant at the news that they were going to have a baby. Keith McCord followed every step of his wife's pregnancy with a mixture of concern and delight, but he was awestruck when he laid his hand on her swollen belly and for the first time felt the movement of a tiny foot or elbow – he was never sure which – pushing against the outer wall of its warm, dark haven. Both scans were inconclusive about the child's sex, and they had joked that whatever it was, they had produced a little troublemaker.

The small bedroom was turned into a nursery, and after work, Keith painted it pale green and decorated it with stencilled farm animals and flowers. They might live in an urban dump, but his child would grow up loving nature. He could not wait for the moment he would be able to show his child this wonderful world.

And then, after a whirl of excitement, he had found himself by his wife's side, holding her hand while she was pushing and trying to breathe through the pain. He winced at the strength of her grip during each contraction but after pushing for twenty hours in vain, her grip slackened; a senior midwife checked how things were progressing and shook her head; a doctor came, felt her pulse and announced in a flat voice that the patient would be taken to the theatre because there were complications. Keith squeezed his wife's hand helplessly before she was wheeled away, smiling weakly at him. A young nurse appeared and steered the reluctant Keith to a waiting room where he was provided with tea and toast, which he left untouched.

After what seemed an eternity, the same doctor entered the room with a gloomy expression on his face. Keith heard him speak as if through a dense fog, refusing to take in anything he said.

Having delivered the devastating news, the doctor fled and left it to the nurse to lead the shell-shocked widower to the room where he had last seen his wife. Her things were still there: her dressing gown on the bed, her cheap but pretty watch on the bedside table, her overnight bag on the floor.

He was still staring at the carefully ironed and folded clothes that she had planned to wear during her confinement and the tiny white Babygros when one of the midwives appeared, carrying a tightly wrapped bundle. She placed it gently in his arms but kept one of her arms underneath as if afraid he might drop it.

Big eyes in a pink, monkey-like face topped with almost black hair tried to focus on him. The puckered lips made a sucking sound.

"You've got a beautiful, healthy baby boy," the nurse said.

And for a brief, terrible moment, he wanted to take the ugly little wretch that had killed his young, vibrant wife and wring its scrawny neck. But then the creature took a deep breath, scrunched up its face that turned purple in an instant, and made a pathetic wailing sound.

"He needs his bottle," the midwife said. "Sit down. I'll show you."

Deeply ashamed, Keith obeyed, and only when his son began to suckle furiously, screwing up his eyes in delight, did the tears begin to flow and drip onto the snow-white blanket.

And so, Russell McCord came into the world, set on his path to atone for his original sin by hunting down and punishing those who had taken an innocent life.

* * *

McCord, with all that family history heavy on his mind, entered the stairwell where the familiar odours of urine and bleach were fighting for supremacy, and climbed up to the first floor flat. He was thinking of his dad's steadfast refusal to accept some of his savings and move into a nicer part of town closer to McCord's own flat in Portobello. Keith McCord had clung on to the ever more idealistic memory of his dead wife until he met Clare and discovered that the past can be cherished without sacrificing the present and the future.

Initially, McCord had not been enamoured with the idea of a strange female invading the space that had always been his and his dad's alone, but over the past year he had come to appreciate the happiness she had brought into Keith's life. More importantly, however, Clare, being a wise woman, had not stood in the way of the men's sacred curry-and-chess night.

He shouldered open the door that had been left slightly ajar in anticipation of his arrival and carried the bag full of fragrant takeaway dishes into the tiny kitchen where his dad stood, beaming.

"Great to see you, Russell."

Keith squeezed his shoulder, which had always been the understated manifestation of the deep love he felt for his son.

Clare came through and gave him a big hug before he even had time to put the bag down. She smelled nice, as usual, and exuded warmth and homeliness. He and his dad, despite being very close, had never been very physical, and McCord was still getting used to Clare's comparatively exuberant expressions of affection.

Keith took the bag and began to unwrap poppadom and naan breads before spooning meat and sauce onto the heated plates.

Clare saw to the drinks, and soon they were sitting at the small table in the corner of the living room overlooked by the photograph of his mother that had stood on the mantelpiece ever since he could remember. McCord wondered how Clare felt about that but, of course, he would never ask. Whenever Keith mentioned her, which was often, she seemed perfectly relaxed about it. He marvelled at people who naturally formed happy relationships, and his admiration was tinged with jealousy. For him, these things had never been easy.

"Have you heard about the fire on Ravelston Dykes Road?" Clare asked. "The papers are full of it. Imagine, losing all your possessions!"

"I doubt they lost much at all," McCord said. "The owner is already planning to put underfloor heating in when the house is rebuilt."

"How do you know? There was speculation in the papers that there was a body in there, but was it murder?" Keith asked.

McCord knew that whatever he said in this room would go no further and, in the past, his dad had proved to be an excellent listener to bounce ideas off of.

"Yes, there was a body, the wife of the owner. We got the confirmation this morning. There are clear indications that it was arson, so it is now a murder investigation. No doubt Superintendent Gilchrist will make an official announcement tomorrow, and then the media circus will start right and proper. The initial suspect was a tomcat, but a nine-year-old boy has proven him innocent."

Naturally, Keith and Clare wanted to know more, and so, to their great amusement, McCord related the whole story. He knew, however, that all this chatter simply delayed the inevitable questioning about his own private life. And right enough, there it was.

"By the way," Keith said as if this had just occurred to him now, "is your Amy back yet from her travels across Europe?"

McCord sighed.

"Dad, for the hundredth time, she is not *my* Amy, and yes, she is back sticking her nose into my investigations. She is still Gilchrist's pet and treats the station as her second home."

"Now don't you pretend that you didn't miss her when she was away on the Continent," Keith said with a wry smile.

McCord grimaced. "Like a recurring toothache."

"Nonsense. You two are a great team, and without her you would not have solved your last high-profile cases. No, no, no" – Keith waved away his protestations – "you told me so yourself at the time."

"Whatever," McCord said, desperate to move the conversation away from Amy. "I've actually met another very nice girl in the course of this investigation."

"Really?" Keith sounded sceptical. "And who is that?"

"The gardener at Roseburn House. She is pretty, as well. I might ask her out when the case is closed."

"I'll believe that when I see it," Keith muttered.

"You're a fine one to talk," he countered heatedly.

Clare put down her fork with unusual force.

"Stop it, you two," she said. "Keith, you leave Russell alone. It is entirely his business whom he asks out – or not, as the case may be. And you, Russell, show respect for your father. Grief affects people differently. You have never dealt with your grief and feelings of guilt either. Maybe you should get some professional help. There are some great–"

"Are you suggesting I'm mentally ill?" McCord said in a low voice that was much feared by colleagues and criminals alike.

"Of course not." Clare sighed. "But you two are still stuck in the twentieth century with your attitudes to mental health. Even Prince William–"

"Prince William!" McCord and his dad snorted in unison and laughed.

Having achieved her aim of reconciling father and son, Clare boxed them both playfully in the arm. "Dessert, anyone?"

Chapter 8

"DC Sutton has come up with some very interesting information about Morton Fisher," McCord told his team during the following morning's briefing. "There are indications that Fisher has been using his betting shops as a front for money laundering. It is quite possible that this is what Victoria Norval referred to when she threatened to tell the world what a villain he was. I also had a phone call this morning from our youngest member of staff" – McCord waited until the wave of mirth had passed through the large open-plan office as everybody knew about Hunter McLellan by now – "and he told me that on the day of the fire, Norval was secretly going through papers in her husband's study and took away a notebook of some kind. It's quite possible that this was when she found out about his criminal activities and decided to expose him.

Unfortunately, the fire will have destroyed the notebook and all the papers related to his affairs."

"Unless," Calderwood said, "she removed them to a safe place. She wouldn't have threatened him with exposure without keeping evidence, would she?"

"Good point," McCord said, "but where would she have hidden them? Maybe at the boyfriend's? We need to speak to him anyway because she might have told him something about her husband's dodgy dealings."

"What about the victim's stepchildren? Does either of them have a motive?" Calderwood asked.

McCord looked around the room until his eyes fastened on PC Dharwan's exquisite face. He always marvelled at how she could remain so serene while doing such a demanding job. She raised her hand and McCord motioned her to speak.

"I've been doing some research into Patrick Fisher. He is Fisher's son from a previous marriage. His mother died of cancer six years ago. No convictions, a caution five years ago for possession but nothing since. He has had no regular job since leaving Heriot-Watt's with a degree in Creative Writing. The sole product of this so far is a sci-fi novel called *The Deadly Planet*, which he self-published three years ago without much success. He was staying at Roseburn House and has been living on an allowance from his father."

McCord nodded.

"Thank you, PC Dharwan. According to the housekeeper, Victoria Norval had persuaded her husband to stop Patrick's allowance, so she was not his favourite person."

"I wonder if Patrick is involved in his father's criminal activities," Calderwood said. "It would be an easy way to make money since being a writer is rarely a lucrative profession, and certainly not in his case."

"That's a possibility," McCord agreed. "He was terribly quick to tell everybody that his stepmother was not in the burning house and point the finger at her as the arsonist. Maybe father and son were in this together? Patrick could have run to Roseburn House and back much more quickly than his father. What do we know about Patrick's sister, Danielle?"

PC Mike Turner stood up, ran his fingers through his tousled hair and attempted to straighten his creased tie.

McCord would have reprimanded any other officer for such a sloppy appearance, but Turner was a bright spark and, more importantly, he had the hunting instinct. He reminded McCord a little of himself when he started off; apart from the fact, of course, that McCord had always been well turned out.

Turner cleared his throat. "Like her brother, Danielle was educated at George Watson's. By all accounts a quiet girl who never put a foot wrong, unlike Patrick. After leaving school, she trained as a beautician and then married a guy called Stuart McLellan. He is quite a bit older than her and works for the Financial Conduct Authority. He's been with the FCA since he graduated from Glasgow University with a First in Economics. Neither Danielle nor Stuart is on file for anything. They have a son, as we all know, called Hunter. That's all, I'm afraid."

He sat down again.

"Thank you, PC Turner," McCord said. "I suppose both Patrick and Danielle have a motive, but in each case it is weak. Although they didn't get on very well with their stepmother, they don't stand to inherit, unless Morton Fisher pops his clogs soon, and Norval didn't threaten them with anything before the fire as far as we know."

McCord tapped on Morton Fisher's picture on the incident board.

"No, my bet is on the husband, so let's concentrate on him. If Morton Fisher, or anybody else for that matter, went back to the house in a hurry, somebody must have seen them. I want a door-to-door all along the way between Roseburn House and the restaurant and in the streets running parallel as well. PC Turner, I want you and PC Dharwan to get onto that."

"Yes, sir," they answered as one.

"DS Struthers, I want you to contact Fisher's housekeeper, Jennifer Hamill. I've spoken to her already, but now that this is a murder inquiry, we need to get a formal statement and to check her alibi."

"Yes, sir."

"In the meantime, DS Calderwood and I are going to pay a visit to Victoria Norval's grieving boyfriend."

* * *

James Palmer-Wycliffe resided in a modern, three-bedroom flat on Newbattle Terrace. As he opened the door to the two detectives, McCord thought he saw fear flicker across the handsome features, but after a split-second their host recovered the easy confidence that is one of the main benefits of an expensive private education.

Palmer-Wycliffe showed them into a stylish but rather messy living room.

"Please have a seat, officers," Palmer-Wycliffe said, hastily picking up the clothes that had been flung over the back of the sofa.

"What can I do for you?"

"We would like to ask you about your relationship with Victoria Norval," McCord said, placing a printout of Norval's Twitter post on the glass-topped coffee table that had not been wiped recently.

"Ah," Palmer-Wycliffe said. "I had hoped to keep that private. Our respective families would not be keen on the idea of Victoria and me... you know."

Calderwood smiled sympathetically. "Yes, our parents always seem to know better than us who we should be with, don't they?"

McCord could not help nodding vigorously.

"You're so right," Palmer-Wycliffe said, giving Calderwood an appreciative glance.

It never ceased to amaze McCord how Calderwood could manipulate everybody into liking him. Or perhaps that was unfair. Calderwood was simply a very nice guy who instinctively knew how to make people feel relaxed. But now it was time to end the idle chitchat and to get some answers.

"So, what was the deal between the two of you?" McCord asked.

Palmer-Wycliffe regarded him with slight distaste.

"We met occasionally and discreetly, either here or in a hotel. I gave her what her husband could or would not supply. We always had a great time."

Seeing the expression on McCord's face, he added, "We were close, you know? It was not purely about sex."

"Close enough for her to entrust you with evidence incriminating her husband?" McCord asked.

"What?" Palmer-Wycliffe appeared shocked. "Evidence of some sort of crime? No, she never gave me anything of the sort. We never talked about her husband."

McCord tried to hide his disappointment.

"And how did you feel about Ms Norval planning to publicise your affair two days before she died?"

"I was worried about her," Palmer-Wycliffe said.

"Because of what her husband might do?" McCord asked. "Have you ever met Morton Fisher?"

There was the slightest hesitation, then an ironic smile. "No. You wouldn't be keen to come face to face with your lover's husband, would you?"

"But when their house burnt down and you didn't hear from Ms Norval again, did you not think to contact the police?"

"I was hoping that..." He lowered his head.

"We wouldn't figure out it was you?" McCord shot a side glance at Calderwood both admitting to the lie and asking him not to give him away. "Well, you wear very expensive and distinctive suits," he added, enjoying Palmer-Wycliffe's discomfort. McCord could not stand his sort – the over-confident, entitled kind of people who think the world owes them everything they desire.

"Do you know I could charge you with obstruction in a murder inquiry?"

When Palmer-Wycliffe raised his head, the apprehension which had been showing on his face was replaced by arrogance. "I had no idea Vic was murdered. I like to keep private matters private, that's all. I thought the police would be more interested in the arson than in an affair that had nothing whatsoever to do with it."

"That is for us to decide," McCord said with a grim smile. "May we have a look at your phone? There could be something in her messages to you that would help us."

"I assure you, there isn't. And I believe you need a warrant for that," Palmer-Wycliffe said, his voice now glacial.

He rose from his seat, indicating that the meeting was over. "And next time you want to speak to me, I'd appreciate it if you made an appointment so that I can have my solicitor present."

"Don't you worry, we shall do that," McCord said through clenched teeth. "Good day, Mr Palmer-Wycliffe."

Outside, McCord waited for Calderwood to say something, but his partner kept a dogged silence.

"Alright," McCord said, "you think that if I had left the interview to you, he would have handed over the notebook and his phone."

"I don't think he knows anything about the notebook," Calderwood said evenly. "But why was he so defensive about the affair? He is single, as far as we know, isn't he? And did you notice that he seemed almost relieved when we confronted him with the Twitter post? I had the distinct feeling that he was hiding something."

"Me, too," McCord said.

"Maybe Amy has managed to unearth some useful information?" Calderwood suggested.

McCord was not about to grovel. "I'm sure she'll come running as soon as she has news."

Calderwood sighed.

"What?" McCord asked, nettled.

"Don't you think you should give her a little more credit for what she does, sir?"

"And make her even more big-headed? No way. It was her who ran off to swan around Europe for months, remember?"

Calderwood smiled. "You never told me what happened at that Japanese dinner." Seeing the expression on McCord's face, he added, "Of course, it is none of my business."

There was a lengthy silence during which McCord contemplated the fact that Calderwood had been unwaveringly loyal as well as discreet.

"Let's just say, Calderwood, that my palate and Japanese cuisine are incompatible."

"Fair enough," said Calderwood. "It's not my favourite either but then it would be sensible to say that straight away rather than forcing down a dinner you dislike."

"It's easy for you to–"

McCord broke off, remembering the months of pain Calderwood had gone through after the shooting without complaining once that it had seriously hampered his budding romance with PC Surina Dharwan.

"Never mind. Let's concentrate on the case, shall we?" McCord said briskly. "Gilchrist is having anxiety attacks that I might wrongly arrest Morton Fisher for the murder of his wife. We need proof, and pronto."

Chapter 9

The memory of the scars and bruises on Danielle McLellan's thighs had bothered Amy ever since the interview. Violence against women made her very angry, and over the course of the day, she had become more and more determined to do something about it. So, as soon as John came back from a meeting that afternoon, she followed him into his office.

"I'd like to do a feature on domestic violence," she declared. "I've seen enough catwalks to last me a lifetime."

"Where did this idea come from?" he asked.

She was not about to tell him.

"In the past year alone," she said instead, "there were over sixty-four thousand recorded incidents of domestic abuse in Scotland. And that is only the tip of the iceberg. Around eighty percent of those are committed by men on women. Something needs to be done about this. I'd like to interview women who managed to get out of that situation. They might offer good advice to those who are still stuck in an abusive relationship. I could also talk to men, of course, some perpetrators, some victims, er..."

She hesitated, cursing herself for mentioning men, and she was right. A deep frown appeared on John's forehead.

"It is certainly a worthy topic," he said slowly, "but must you always choose subject matters that put you in danger? Your mother will not approve, and she will hold me responsible for anything, and I mean anything, that might happen to you. Needless to say, I don't want anything to happen to you either."

Amy leant across the desk and gave him a kiss on his smooth cheek that smelled pleasantly of aftershave. "You two really do need to stop worrying about me. What on earth do you think might happen? That I drown in the tears of the women I interview?"

"I have serious concerns that the men who are violent towards women anyway might make you the target for their aggression. After all, they will think you are interfering in their private lives and that you might set the police onto them. However," he said, cheering up slightly, "I suppose it is better than chasing a psychopathic arsonist."

Amy was not going to destroy his illusion. "DI McCord is pretty sure he knows who the killer is and therefore he has little use for me at the moment," Amy said. "I'm purely involved in gathering background information on the victim." This, on some level, was entirely true.

Her phone buzzed. She looked at the display with a mischievous grin. "Speak of the devil. Good afternoon, DI McCord. What can I do for you?"

"I am surprised, Miss Thornton, that you haven't been at the station again. Normally, you are difficult to get rid of."

"Oh, I know when I'm not wanted. Are you perhaps stuck in your investigation and requiring my assistance?"

"Not at all. The evidence on Morton Fisher's money laundering is piling up, thanks to DC Sutton. But Calderwood and I have just spoken to James Palmer-Wycliffe. He's admitting to the affair but hasn't given us anything beyond that. Calderwood is wondering if you have found out anything else about him."

Amy smiled to herself. "I thought you were not interested in Palmer-Wycliffe?" she asked innocently.

"He denies any knowledge of a notebook Victoria Norval took from Fisher's study and I think that his relationship with Norval was fairly casual but Calderwood and I both got the distinct impression that he is hiding something."

Amy sighed with pleasure before dropping the bombshell. "Do you think that something could be the fact that he was at the scene of the fire?"

The explosion that followed hit her with unexpected force.

"What?! Palmer-Wycliffe was at the scene of the crime, and you did not think it necessary to inform me?" McCord shouted into the phone. "You know what this is? A criminal offence! Withholding evidence, that is; obstructing an inquiry, that is!"

"Don't you shout at me!" she said indignantly. "You are the one who told me that Morton Fisher was your man."

She heard him breathe deeply in and out trying to calm himself down. "How did you find out he was there? Palmer-Wycliffe did not admit to it, did he?"

"I haven't had the opportunity to speak to him yet," Amy said, "but Chloe Chalmers, the gardener, said that she saw him. He was standing at the gate watching the house burn down. 'Mesmerised' was the word she used. What did Palmer-Wycliffe say to you?"

"Nothing. He got stroppy when I asked to see his phone and he mentioned contacting a lawyer if we insist on seeing it. Either he is sensitive about his privacy, or he has something to hide. He probably thinks Norval's phone was destroyed by the fire but we're hoping that forensics can retrieve some of the content."

"You might be better to wait for that before you speak to him again," Amy said.

McCord growled. "Thanks for telling me how to do my job."

"You're welcome. I'll see what I can find out about him," she added, more conciliatory. As much as she enjoyed sparring with McCord, she hated falling out with him. "Will you let me know what turns up from Norval's phone?"

"You've got a nerve to ask," McCord said.

"Can I come with you then when you interview Palmer-Wycliffe?" Amy asked pleadingly.

"Don't be ridiculous," McCord said and hung up.

As the line went dead, Amy stomped her foot in frustration, but then she saw the expression on John's face.

"Purely involved in gathering background information, are you?" He put his head in his hands as if it suddenly had become too heavy.

"Please, John, don't tell Mum," Amy pleaded. "We had an argument about that already, and she needs some time to digest the fact that I'm not going to stop investigating crimes."

She sidled up to him, put her arms round his shoulders and kissed the parting of his perfectly cut salt-and-pepper hair.

"It would be much kinder if you don't tell her, and as far as I'm concerned, you, of course, had no idea what I was up to. I was always a wayward child, and we all know that you are much too sweet to suspect me of doing anything naughty."

John lifted his head.

"Thanks very much. Now I'm going to be a liar as well as naïve."

"Not saying everything is not lying," Amy said. "As a magazine editor, you of all people should know that."

John shook his head. "Sometimes I wonder why we are concerned about you at all. I'm beginning to think DI McCord needs protecting from you, not the other way round."

Amy laughed. "There you could well be right."

Chapter 10

The following morning, McCord called PC Turner into his Sunset Boulevard. The young constable grinned as he entered the office. "You should get a beach chair in here, sir, and a drinks cabinet."

"Dream on," McCord said. "Anything on the house-to-house?"

"The next-door neighbour was working in the garden and saw them all leave for the restaurant, everyone, that is, apart from Danielle McLellan. She left later and the neighbour says she was shouting into her phone."

McCord frowned. "But she couldn't have started the fire, could she? She didn't know at that point that Norval would come home early."

"That's what I thought as well, sir," Turner said. "Unfortunately, nobody saw any members of the household on the streets between the house and the restaurant before they all returned. We checked all along Ravelston Dykes Road in case somebody noticed anything suspicious around the time of the fire, but we found nothing. It doesn't help that the properties next to Roseburn House are mostly surrounded either by a wall or a high hedge. They also have large front gardens, so the residents don't necessarily see who is walking on the pavement."

There was a perfunctory knock on the door, and Calderwood rushed in, all excited.

"Sir, forensics have recovered some of Norval's phone messages," he said. "And guess what? Palmer-Wycliffe broke off with her the day before the fire. Isn't it interesting that he failed to mention that when we spoke to him?"

McCord grabbed the printouts and started to read through them. "Norval didn't take it too well then. 'How can you do that to me... I loved you... I wanted your children... You've ruined my life, and you'll regret this!' That was the day after her Twitter post."

"So, it looks like Amy was right; he did not want to make their relationship public," Calderwood said. "Instead, he broke up with her. Of course, it could just be that it was all getting too serious for him if he was only after the sex."

"But then he turns up at the scene of the fire in which Victoria Norval dies," McCord said. "We need to get a formal statement from the gardener, and then we'll bring Mr Palmer-Wycliffe in for another chat."

McCord could easily have found Chloe Chalmers's phone number and asked her to come into the station. He could also have sent a junior officer out to Roseburn House, but for some reason he did neither of those things. Instead, he felt like taking a little trip out to Ravelston to watch her plant shrubs. His office window was wide open, letting in the hum of passing traffic. Warm morning air was wafting over from Calton Hill with its National Monument, which, although intended as an exact copy of the Acropolis, had never progressed beyond twelve columns. On such rare occasions, McCord understood why somebody had once called Edinburgh the Athens of the North.

McCord rummaged in his desk drawer for the witness statement forms, pulled out a couple and put them in a folder along with a pen.

"I'm off to Roseburn House. I won't be long," he told Calderwood, who looked bemused at his boss's unnecessary journey through the congested city centre.

Leaving his jacket behind, something which one does on very few days of the year in Scotland's capital city, McCord headed out into the hazy sunshine.

* * *

Around the same time, Amy was walking back and forth on Corstorphine Road, waiting for an opportunity to speak to Danielle McLellan in private. The heat from the tarmac was permeating the thin soles of her dainty sandals whose leather straps were beginning to chafe on her ankles. Most of the morning she had been here, but Danielle had not left The Braemar at all, not even for a little bit of shopping. If that woman had any sense at all, of course, she would be sitting down with a cool drink, which was what Amy now decided to do, even if it risked her being seen by Danielle's father or brother. She turned into the driveway of the hotel and wandered around the garden, casually approaching the shielded patios, and listening for familiar voices.

A waiter hurried towards her across the lawn. Was he going to question her about what she was doing here when she wasn't a guest? It was too late to avoid him without causing suspicion, so Amy decided to brazen it out and claim to have been invited by the Fisher family. She was sure Hunter at least would be happy to see her if no one else. But having reached her, the waiter merely announced that unfortunately all the patios were taken at present and asked if she would enjoy a drink inside.

On entering the lobby, she spotted an armchair half covered by a gumtree and with a sigh of relief let herself sink into the cool leather. She inspected the unsightly blisters on the back of her ankles and cursed herself for not carrying plasters in her handbag, something her mother had always admonished her to do. Before she had a chance to reflect on how her mother had always given her excellent advice on everything apart from relationships, she was presented with a colourful mocktail and that day's edition of *The Times*. Sadly, it was not the broadsheet size it had once been when it had helped generations of spies to do their surveillance work undetected, but the paper still afforded reasonable cover in an emergency.

Amy had savoured the first, delicious sip of the fruity fizz when Danielle McLellan stepped out of the lift and made her way towards the exit. Cursing under her breath, Amy gave her a minute's start, left a banknote on the table, hoping that it would cover the cost of her drink, and followed Fisher's daughter outside.

Danielle McLellan was hurrying along the driveway towards the gate, but the closer it came, the more slowly she walked until she finally stopped next to the preposterous gold-painted lions flanking the entrance. She looked down Corstorphine Road, first left, then right. She took a deep breath and seemed to make up her mind to go but then thought better of it, turned round and almost bumped into Amy.

"So sorry," Danielle McLellan gasped, steadying herself on Amy's outstretched arm.

"Are you okay?" Amy asked. "Can I help you in any way?"

It was only now that Danielle McLellan recognised her.

"You are that journalist who came to interview us. What are you doing here? Go away!" Her voice, rather than being assertive, was bordering on the hysterical.

"Listen," Amy said urgently, "I've seen your bruises and the burn marks on your thighs. I can help you."

"I don't need help, not from a reporter, anyway. But my son…" Danielle McLellan began to sob.

"What's happened to Hunter?" Amy asked, suddenly anxious herself. "Where is he?"

"I don't know, he's gone off somewhere, again, although I've told him…" The tears were running freely now.

"I'm sure Hunter is fine," Amy said, trying to sound calm. "He is quite streetwise. Where do you think he might have gone?"

"Probably to Roseburn House to see that gardener; he goes there every day although I keep telling him not to."

Amy breathed a sigh of relief.

"He'll be quite safe with her; she is a nice girl. Why don't we go there together and find him?"

Danielle McLellan's relief was palpable. "Thank you."

They had been walking for a while in silence when Amy could hold back no longer. "There is help out there, Danielle. Things don't need to be like that even if you find it hard to believe. There are safe houses you can go to…"

"Surely, I'm safe with my father?" Danielle McLellan snapped.

"Of course," Amy hastily agreed. "But you should report whoever is doing this to you. I assume, it is your husband?"

Danielle McLellan said nothing but simply walked faster so that Amy had difficulty keeping up with her high heels and raw ankles. But then she thought of the circular scar tissue on Danielle's thighs and pushed her own pain aside.

"I know some really nice policemen who would listen to you," she said.

"No, thank you, I met one of them recently. He treated us all like murder suspects."

Typical McCord, Amy thought, always in there with the subtlety of a wrecking ball.

"That's because he was investigating a murder. What is happening to you is completely different. You are the victim here, remember? You could speak to PC Dharwan first, she is very kind."

Danielle McLellan suddenly stopped. "Why do you keep badgering me? You're only after a story. All I want is to find my son and get back to the hotel!"

"I was only trying to help," Amy said, hurt that her genuine concern was misconstrued.

After ten more agonising minutes walking in silence, they finally arrived at Roseburn House, both women sweating from the heat and the exertion, Amy limping and conscious of the warm blood running down the back of her heels. I am going to wear Crocs next time, she told herself but knew even then that she was kidding herself.

The driveway of Roseburn House seemed a mile long, but eventually they reached the back of the destroyed house and sweet, cool shade. Amy's delight, however, was short-lived. In front of them, at a roughly hewn wooden table laid with a jug of home-made lemonade and glasses, sat Chloe Chalmers in the company of Hunter and McCord who, after the initial surprise had passed, looked quite pleased with himself.

With a little shriek, Danielle McLellan grabbed her son by the shoulders and shook him. "What did I tell you about sneaking out of the hotel? Do you have any idea how worried I've been?"

Then she stopped, took a deep breath and embraced him.

Hunter hugged her back before wriggling free. "I'm fine, Mum. Sit down and have a drink. You look terrible."

Amy saw that McCord barely managed to suppress a grin and, conscious of the way she must appear herself, turned her anger on him.

"Did it not occur to either of you to let the family know where Hunter was?" she said, looking accusingly not at Chalmers but at McCord.

"Hunter is quite a regular visitor here," Chloe said. "I assumed you knew, Mrs McLellan. I'm very sorry if you were worried. Let me get you a drink."

She stood up to fetch some more glasses from the nearby garden house.

Amy and Danielle McLellan sat down heavily on one of the benches.

"Everything okay?" McCord asked Amy, demonstratively taking in her lacklustre appearance and the ankles that had little rivulets of blood running down their back. "That must be sore."

"It is," Amy said shortly.

She had spied the witness statement form on the table and gave McCord a look that implied, 'And?'

McCord simply shrugged imperceptibly.

"Hunter," he said with as much authority as he could muster, "I need to speak to your mother in private. Off you go. Play for a while in the garden."

With an expression of utter disgust on his face, Hunter edged away from the table at the very moment Chloe Chalmers reappeared and poured some lemonade for the new arrivals. Amy's mouth began to water at the crackling sound of the ice cubes in the cold, fizzy drink.

Chloe handed both a glass with a smile that told them she understood the situation. "Come on, Hunter," she said, "let's see if somebody new has moved into the bug hotel."

Hunter merely rolled his eyes in contempt at the feeble pretence but followed her into the wilderness that the back garden was developing into.

McCord waited until they were out of earshot. "Mrs McLellan," he said, "at our last conversation I had the impression that you were holding something back.

Maybe here, away from... other people, you feel more comfortable now about speaking to me?"

Danielle McLellan chewed fiercely on her compostable straw but said nothing.

McCord tried again.

"There is mounting evidence that your father had motive to kill your stepmother. Her ex-boyfriend was here during the fire. I know you and Ms Norval were not the best of friends but please remember: a woman has been murdered, and obstructing a police inquiry is a criminal offence."

At that, Danielle McLellan broke into hysterical laughter. "Are you threatening me?" she gasped, as if that was the funniest thing that had happened to her in a while.

Amy glanced reproachfully at McCord.

When Danielle McLellan had calmed down a little, she looked McCord straight in the eye. "Daddy would never kill anybody, and I know nothing about Victoria's boyfriend. Patrick told me when I arrived that he was sure she was having an affair but then, he hated her so much, he always thought the worst of her." Suddenly realising what she had said, she dropped her glass so hard on the table that it threatened to crack. "I didn't mean to say that he–"

"And why did Patrick hate her so much?" McCord asked, ignoring her protestations.

"She tried to turn Daddy against him," Danielle McLellan said. "He was quite happy supporting Patrick while he was pursuing his 'writing career'" – a little sneer appeared around the corner of her mouth – "but then Victoria persuaded Daddy that Patrick needed to learn to stand on his own feet and that it wasn't healthy for a man in his thirties to be living at home. We all knew she was after Daddy's money, of course."

"I see," McCord said.

Danielle McLellan stood up.

"Hunter and I are going back to the hotel now," she said, "unless you are going to arrest me."

"No need for that at the moment," McCord said, his tone leaving it open for interpretation whether he was joking or not. "But please don't leave the area without notifying us."

Danielle McLellan emitted one of her shrieking laughs again.

"Will you be okay walking back on your own?" Amy asked, pointing to her feet. "I don't think I can do one more step in these."

Danielle McLellan hesitated, then pulled herself up to her full height. "I won't be on my own," she said, suddenly dignified. "I'll have my son with me. Hunter! Come on, we're going to be late for lunch. Today's special is fajitas."

Hunter showed no enthusiasm to leave, but the prospect of food seemed to deflect him from an open revolt.

"Goodbye, DI McCord; goodbye, miss," he said very formally. "I'm sure we'll meet again soon. See you, Chloe."

He gave her a quick hug that seemed to surprise everybody apart from the gardener.

"Be good," she called after him as he disappeared with his mother round the corner.

McCord slid the witness statement into the folder.

"Thanks again, Chloe," he said, "you were very helpful."

Amy frowned. Chloe, is it? she wondered.

Chalmers hesitated. "Is what I said going to make that man a murder suspect? I wouldn't want somebody who is probably perfectly innocent to be accused because of me. I saw him only on that one occasion, and at that time, the fire was already raging."

"We don't throw people into the dungeon on the say-so of one witness alone, however perceptive she might be," McCord said with a little bow towards her. "If we arrest him, we will have very good reason to. Your statement, as valuable as it is, will be just one piece of the puzzle, so please don't worry."

Amy gnawed on her lip. Could that really be McCord flirting? He had certainly never spoken to her like that. Amy looked at the creamy, freckled skin of the woman opposite her. One could find the freckles cute, possibly, and when she smiled, her green eyes shone like precious stones. Ginger-haired people were often the butt of jokes, but Chalmers's waves cascaded beautifully down her arms that were quite muscular and contrasted with the fragility suggested by her features.

"Do you really think he could be the killer?" Chalmers asked with a little shudder.

"To be perfectly honest, I don't think so," McCord said. "His motive is unclear. Other people had much more reason to kill her."

"You are thinking of Mr Fisher, aren't you?" Chalmers quite unnecessarily placed the pen back in McCord's hand, and Amy noticed that their fingers brushed against each other.

"You're not exactly rushing to defend him," McCord said. It was more a statement than a question. "Can you see him as somebody who would set his own house on fire to kill his wife?"

Chalmers seemed to ponder this. "I wouldn't be surprised to hear that he is completely ruthless where his own interests are concerned. But to kill his wife like that, even if she was betraying him? No, but then, I can't imagine that of anybody."

McCord nodded as if this confirmed what he had thought, not of Fisher but of Chalmers.

"Are you not afraid of being out here on your own?" he asked.

Chalmers shook her head. "Amongst all these" – she made a gesture encompassing the trees around her – "I never feel alone."

McCord was about to say something when his mobile rang.

"Calderwood, what's up?"

He listened intently, and a big grin spread across his face. "Brilliant. I'll be there asap."

He slid his phone back into his trouser pocket and looked regretfully at Chalmers.

"I'm sorry, there has been a development. I'll have to go back to the station."

He picked up the folder and turned to Amy. "Do you need a lift home?"

After the way he had treated her, she would normally have told him in no uncertain terms to get lost, but the thought of making her way across town on public transport in those shoes did not appeal.

"Okay," she said condescendingly. "Thank you for the lemonade, Chloe."

Chalmers smiled. "You're very welcome."

As Amy rose from her seat, her ankles, far from recovered, smarted more than ever. But she was in no mood to concede any weakness. Waving away McCord's proffered arm, she hobbled with clenched teeth towards the gates, silently praying that McCord's Juke would be parked nearby. To her great relief, it was. Having been left in the sun, it was thirty-five degrees inside the car, but she was not going to complain.

"So, what news does Duncan have?" she asked, her curiosity as ever greater than her pride.

McCord fastened his seatbelt and started the engine.

"They've recovered more data from Norval's phone – among other things, some photographs. Calderwood wouldn't tell me what they are of; he says I need to see them for myself. Sometimes I hate the guy."

"No, you don't," Amy said. "And by the way, I don't want you to do a detour on my behalf. Why don't I come to the station with you, and then Mum can pick me up from there, or I'll take a taxi home."

McCord shook his head with a mixture of amusement and exasperation. "But not until you've seen the photographs, right?"

Amy shrugged but said nothing. Sometimes McCord was not quite as clueless as he seemed.

"Was there anything new in Chalmers's statement?" she asked as they made their way at a snail's pace through the afternoon traffic at Haymarket.

McCord shook his head. "She confirmed what she had already told you. When she got back from her walk and found the house on fire, James Palmer-Wycliffe was standing at the gate, watching. I'm surprised that you didn't notice him."

Amy, interpreting this as yet another slight at her lack of professionalism, bristled. "I was trying to identify the family members and observe their reactions," she snapped. "Palmer-Wycliffe was just one in a crowd of other onlookers. How was I supposed to know he was Norval's boyfriend?"

"I didn't say you were."

A bad-tempered silence followed. The car was like an oven. Opening the windows had brought little relief, and obviously it had not occurred to McCord to switch on the air conditioning. But Amy knew she was there only on sufferance, so she did not want to antagonise McCord any further by making demands. She stole a glance across and thought that he looked exhausted. As the sweat was trickling down her neck, she fervently hoped that the good news at the station would improve McCord's mood.

Chapter 11

A heat-induced lethargy had spread through the station. It was stuffy in the open-plan office despite the windows being tilted as far as safety regulations allowed. Officers were sprawled across their desk chairs, sleeves rolled up and ties loosened or discarded. Only PC Dharwan was properly attired; whether she was more impermeable to the temperatures, or her unshakeable self-discipline demanded it, McCord was not sure. At their boss's reappearance, everyone scrambled around fixing their uniforms, trying to look busy, apart from Dharwan, of course, who was quietly working away on her computer, and Calderwood, who was manifestly bursting to impart his news.

McCord waved him into the Sunset Boulevard, which was even more airless than the rest of the station.

Amy, who on the long journey from the car park had almost regretted her decision not to go home and put up her tortured feet, forgot all her pain when Calderwood placed a series of photos on the desk.

Both Amy and McCord studied them silently for a full minute before McCord broke the silence.

"I don't understand what exactly is going on there. Are these photographs that Norval took herself?" he asked.

Calderwood nodded, pacing up and down. "Taken the day before the fire, the same day Palmer-Wycliffe broke up with her. She must have followed him from his flat, thinking he was off to see a new lover and she discovered much more than she'd expected."

Calderwood pointed to the first photograph. "This is Palmer-Wycliffe entering the building where an old schoolfriend of his lives." Seeing McCord's surprise, he smiled. "Norval helpfully also took a shot of the street sign and the house number. I went to Sutton" – he paused as if expecting acknowledgement of his bravery, which was not forthcoming – "and in no time at all, she found for me the occupant's name and his link to Palmer-Wycliffe. The guy is on our system for possession."

McCord smiled at the pride in Calderwood's voice. Why could the others not grasp that all you needed to do to get on with Sutton was to respect her need for solitude? And not to have any dodgy money in your own accounts, of course.

"I then got in touch with the drug squad," Calderwood continued, "and they told me that there has been a surge in crack cocaine use in the area. Ten dead so far – probably as a result of too much ammonia in the mix, but they can't be certain. They also can't figure out where the stuff is coming from. I have a feeling they'll find a little lab in the basement of that building… Look more closely! Palmer-Wycliffe is carrying what seems to be an empty holdall." Calderwood pointed to the next picture. "Here he comes out again, but now with a stuffed holdall. And where do you think we see him next?" He pointed to the third photograph. "At one of Morton Fisher's betting shops. He goes in with the full holdall and leaves later with an empty one."

"Let me get this straight," Amy said, flabbergasted. "Norval's ex-boyfriend is laundering drug money through Fisher's betting shops? And Norval found out and decided to blow the lid on the whole operation? That surely gave him one hell of a motive to kill her."

"Him and Fisher," McCord pointed out. "The important question is, which of them was it?"

Calderwood scooped up the photographs. "Maybe they were both in it together."

"Well," McCord said, "let's ask them, shall we?"

Calderwood's smile evaporated.

"We can't," he said.

McCord looked up.

"What? Whyever not?"

"DCI Baxter from the drug squad phoned back a few minutes before you arrived. He says to back off from Fisher and Palmer-Wycliffe; they want to keep them under surveillance a little longer so they can lift the whole gang."

McCord banged his fist on the table. "Hell, I will. I've got a murder investigation to run, and those two are my prime suspects. I'm not going to sit here twiddling my thumbs until the drug squad get their act together. After all, we are doing their job for them as it is. I'm off to interview Fisher again, and then our Mr Palmer-Wycliffe. It's time we rattled their cage a little."

"But, sir," Calderwood almost shouted, "you can't go around ignoring direct orders from a superior officer!"

"I can't ignore what I don't know," McCord said with a wink. "Unfortunately, you were unable to pass on this latest development before I had done my interviews."

Calderwood sighed. "I don't like this one little bit. If you don't come up with a breakthrough soon, they'll–"

"They'll blame it on me, so don't worry."

Amy cleared her throat. "I could come with you and try to wheedle something out of Patrick Fisher if he is there? He might be more forthcoming to me with the truth about his father. I have my ways..."

"I know you do," McCord grudgingly admitted. "But your feet–"

"My feet are fine," Amy said. "Let's go!"

* * *

Opening the carved wooden door to his Braemar suite, Morton Fisher was no more welcoming now than he had been during McCord's last visit, but his arrogance seemed somewhat contrived this time. His ruddy face was grey, his skin covered in a thin film of sweat.

McCord's sympathy, however, was limited, and he decided to press home his advantage.

"As you will have heard, we are now officially investigating your wife's murder and have found, let's say, irregularities in your financial transactions. Considering that you are at the top of my list of suspects, I was wondering if you would like to expand on your previous statement," McCord said.

Fisher's grip around his cognac glass tightened. McCord wondered how anybody could drink spirits on a sweltering afternoon like this, but he suspected that Fisher's relationship with Prince Hubert was much more intense than the one he had shared with his wife.

"I didn't set fire to my own house. God knows I wanted to kill Vic that evening, but I didn't."

McCord noted the fact that Fisher did not deny his accusations regarding his financial affairs.

"We believe your wife uncovered some criminal aspects of your business and was about to expose you, as she threatened in front of your family and guests during your birthday party. That gives you a very strong motive," McCord said.

Fisher's eyes darted backwards and forwards. McCord could see him agonising over what to say. Had Palmer-Wycliffe warned him about the photos Norval had taken? They probably thought that the fire had destroyed the phone. They could not be sure, however, that Norval had not stored them elsewhere where they might be discovered. At least, Fisher had to assume that the police had not found out about them yet, or he would have been arrested straight away.

McCord wished he could reveal what they knew about the drug operation, but he did not fancy a disciplinary hearing with Gilchrist on the panel. All he could do was make vague threats. Still, for Fisher it must feel like sitting on a time bomb, a thought that filled McCord with uncharitable glee.

"Are you missing a notebook by any chance?" McCord asked.

Fisher frowned. "My diary, address book and all my papers were destroyed in the fire," he said. "Damn nuisance. Why?"

"It seems your wife took a notebook from your study. Did you notice that it was missing?"

"No, I didn't," Fisher snapped.

"You do realise that judges pass more lenient sentences on defendants who are cooperative and show remorse?"

"Stop treating me like a common criminal," Fisher shouted. "I've lost my home!"

McCord did not feel obliged to express any degree of sorrow.

"And what about Mr Palmer-Wycliffe?" McCord asked.

Fisher's eyes widened. "What about him?" he asked in a croaky voice.

"I'm asking you. The name is familiar to you, isn't it? How do you know him?"

"I don't know him. I might have heard his name before. Is he in the betting business?"

"In the widest sense," McCord said, watching Fisher closely. "When did you find out he was your wife's lover?"

For a fleeting second, surprise showed on Fisher's face, but he quickly recovered. "Isn't that immaterial now?"

"I'm surprised you're not asking me to investigate him," McCord said. "He was seen at the scene of the fire.

Don't you think my colleagues and I should look more closely at his affairs?"

Fisher closed his eyes and took a swig at his Prince Hubert.

"Surely, you don't want me to tell you how to do your job," he said eventually. "All I can say is that I didn't kill my wife, so you can't possibly have any proof. I think you should leave now. I've got terrible heartburn and I'm not feeling well. Must be something I've eaten."

McCord was inclined to believe him. The greyness of his complexion was now tinged with a shade of green.

"Well, I hope next time we meet you feel better," he said insincerely. "I reckon, we'll see each other again sooner than you might think."

* * *

Very soon after her arrival at The Braemar, Amy had tracked down Patrick Fisher. Rather than hobbling about in her bloodstained sandals searching for him, she had generously tipped a waiter after convincing him that he was aiding a budding romance.

Patrick Fisher was lying with his eyes closed on one of the deckchairs that the hotel had provided for guests who wanted to enjoy this unprecedented sunny spell in the garden.

When Amy's shadow fell on him, he opened his eyes and stared at her as if she was an apparition. "What are you doing here?"

"Sorry to disturb you, Patrick," Amy warbled. "Were you plotting your next novel?"

Patrick Fisher sat up and gave a quick laugh that did not reach his eyes.

"I think everybody is in agreement that my efforts as a writer are wasted," he said, trying but failing to sound light-hearted.

He looked around but all the other seats were taken. He swivelled his legs to the side and invitingly patted the lower end of his deckchair. Amy did not need to be told twice. She sat down, hiding her unsightly ankles under the wooden frame.

A slight breeze had come up, easing the oppressive atmosphere.

"Would you like a drink? G&T?" he asked.

Amy nodded. Patrick Fisher waved to the waiter, who was still hovering around, and ordered a gin and tonic for Amy and a lager for himself.

"You mustn't give up because your first novel has not brought the rip-roaring success you had dreamed of," Amy said. "Most authors write several novels before their talent is fully appreciated and recognised. And you'll get better each time."

Patrick Fisher's jaw dropped with astonishment.

"What is it?" Amy asked.

"Do you know that you are the first person who has actually encouraged me to do this?"

After a moment, he began to laugh. "But then again, you haven't even read my novel, have you?"

"Fantasy is not my thing," Amy admitted, "but if writing is yours, you should not let it go so easily. Maybe you could try a different genre?"

Patrick Fisher waved that suggestion away dismissively.

"I won't have time now, anyway. My father told me in no uncertain terms that I need to find myself a job and a place of my own."

Pleased that she had him where she wanted, Amy decided to probe a little deeper.

"So, what brought about your father's change of heart?"

Patrick Fisher's face turned crimson.

"Victoria, of course," he said. "As if it was any of her business to intervene. It's obvious she wanted to get as much money out of Dad as possible and didn't want it spent on me. Before she came on the scene, Dad would have a go at me every so often, but in the end, he always let me be. And what am I supposed to do now? With a degree in Creative Writing, you don't exactly get high-powered jobs." Checking himself, he added, "You're not going to write that in one of your articles, are you?"

Amy shook her head. "Of course not."

"By the way, my father wanted my opinion of the draft of your obituary of Victoria. It's very good," Patrick Fisher said. "Very flattering, but then they always are, I suppose."

Suddenly, suspicion crept into his voice. "Why are you here, anyway?"

To Amy's relief, the waiter appeared with their drinks.

"I just fancied a chat," Amy said blithely, "and I was hoping to speak to your sister as well."

"What about?"

Amy hesitated. "How well do you know her husband?"

"Stuart?" Patrick Fisher shrugged. "Not all that well. They've always kept pretty much to themselves. Why?"

"Have you noticed a change in Danielle's behaviour in the last few years?"

Patrick Fisher shrugged again. "Not particularly. Danielle has always been quite nervy, although I do think it has got worse. She probably has too much time on her hands and needs to get herself a job. Hunter is a weekly boarder at Cargilfield, so he is barely at home. I have no idea what she is doing with herself all day. Plumping up cushions, I imagine."

Amy tried not to laugh at the unintended irony in Patrick Fisher's words.

"Has she ever mentioned anything to you about her marriage?"

"No," Patrick Fisher said as if that was an outlandish idea. "We don't get on very well, you see. She is terribly jealous of me. Dad had always wanted a son, and he was disappointed when his first child was a girl. Our mother once told me that and said I should be nicer to my sister."

"Maybe you should," Amy said, not bothering to hide her disapproval. "Have you ever noticed any signs that her husband is abusing her?"

"Abusing her?" Patrick Fisher echoed, incredulous. "As in knocking her about?"

"On the day of our interview, I noticed that there were bruises and marks that look like scars from cigarette burns on her thighs. She also seemed scared of something or somebody when I talked to her this morning."

Patrick Fisher shook his head. "I don't believe that. Stuart is such a... boring chap. I never know what to talk to him about when I see him, which is thankfully rare. And surely Danielle would have said–"

"But would she?" Amy interjected. "You don't seem to be very close as a family."

Patrick Fisher was about to protest, but then slumped against the raised back of the deckchair. "It all went downhill when Mum died of cancer. She was the one who held the family together. After her death, it was everybody for himself. We all became very self-centred."

He seemed lost in thought for a while, then he suddenly frowned.

"Did Danielle tell you about this alleged abuse?"

"Not directly," Amy admitted, "but–"

"I think you are showing far too much interest in our private affairs," he said, all warmth gone from his voice. "You pretend to care for people, so you can exploit them later for your articles. And I fell for it, too. Please leave. And if you print any of this, we'll sue."

Amy, stunned at this sudden change of attitude, rose from her seat with as much dignity as she could muster.

"I'm sorry you feel like that, Patrick. I can assure you–"

"Goodbye," he said with a decisiveness she would not have thought him capable of. "And I strongly suggest you leave my sister alone. She does not need any help from the likes of you."

Amy was tempted to fling her remaining drink at Patrick Fisher's face but managed to restrain herself.

Without another word, she turned to leave. For a second, the pain in her ankles took her breath away but she managed to cross the lawn towards the gate without a limp until she was out of sight from the hotel. When she finally reached McCord's Juke, she leant against its doorframe, but recoiled from the burning hot metal. "Bugger!" she muttered, including in her considered assessment the car, Patrick Fisher, Stuart McLellan and, for good measure, McCord as well.

"Having a good time playing detective?" The sound of McCord's voice right behind her made her jump. "What did Patrick Fisher say?"

Having collected herself, Amy said, "Danielle was right. He did hate Norval and is not overly fond of his old man either. Patrick has no regular income, and he has always been totally dependent on Daddy for his comfortable lifestyle. Until Norval came onto the scene, he was Daddy's golden boy, but Fisher must have seen the light and told the spoiled brat to get himself a job. Patrick claimed that Danielle is not being abused by her husband, but I'm not sure if he is lying or completely clueless."

"Have you considered the possibility that he may be right?" McCord asked as he started the engine and let down all the windows. "She denied the abuse when you suggested it, didn't she?"

Amy jammed the seatbelt into the lock. "She didn't deny it; she refused to talk about it. There is a difference. Tell me, if she isn't a victim of abuse, where do the bruises and scars come from? And what, or rather who, is she afraid of if not her husband?"

"I wonder," McCord said, sliding his phone into the holder below the dashboard. "Maybe she knows that her father killed Norval and is afraid of him? Maybe he made it clear to her that she'd better keep quiet?"

Amy stuck her arm out of the window to catch the cool breeze generated by the movement of the car. "It's possible, but I had the distinct impression that she adores her father. If she knew about any crime of his, I suspect she would protect him anyway. Also, she was afraid to leave the hotel when she went off to find Hunter. If it's her father who scares her, why doesn't she go home to her husband?"

"Good point. Still, Fisher strikes me as a ruthless character. And Chloe Chalmers said so as well."

Amy gave a very unladylike snort.

"Well, if Miss Chalmers says so, it must be true."

McCord kept his eyes on the road, ignoring her outburst. "Morton Fisher is now like a cornered rat; he isn't sure how much we know and what Palmer-Wycliffe might have told us. Fisher probably called him as soon as I left."

Right on cue, McCord's phone rang. Both looked at the display. McCord declined the call.

"But that was Duncan," Amy said. "Why–"

"Calderwood has been unable to pass on the message from DCI Baxter, remember? I'm not answering any calls from him until I've spoken to Palmer-Wycliffe."

"But what if it's important?" Amy asked. "Hang on, I'll call him."

It rang only once before Calderwood picked up. She put him on loudspeaker. "Are you with the boss?" he asked.

"Yes, we're on our way to Palmer-Wycliffe," she said with a mischievous side glance at McCord. "What's happened?"

"I can save you both a journey. Palmer-Wycliffe called a few minutes ago to say he's coming in to make a statement."

"Yes!" McCord banged the steering wheel with delight, which made the car swerve dangerously for a second, provoking a honking of horns behind and next to him. McCord paid no attention to them, grateful not for the first time that he was in his own car and in civilian clothes. "The rats' cage has been well and truly rattled. I bet he's going to give us the low-down on Fisher to save his own neck, and that will be the case solved."

Chapter 12

To McCord's endless frustration, the journey back took over an hour as the teatime traffic inched its way through the city centre. The town was heaving, and the Edinburgh Festival had not even started yet. Tourists craned their necks admiring the sights and stepped inadvertently off pavements. Groups of carefree youngsters insisted on walking side by side although there was not sufficient space for them to do that, causing them to spill over into the road in the optimistic belief of youth that they were immortal. Herds of pedestrians, seeking safety in numbers, crossed the road long after the green man had turned red, and in the airless metal boxes that were lurching spasmodically towards their destination, drivers swore and yet again rued their decision to use their cars in the motorists' hell that is Edinburgh City Centre.

When they eventually reached St Leonard's, McCord had run several yards towards the entrance before he remembered that with her sore ankles Amy was unable to follow at his speed. Awkwardly, he waited and offered her his arm. She took it reluctantly at first, but then her grip tightened around his lower arm as she leant on him for support. He suddenly had a vision of sweeping her up into his arms and carrying her upstairs to his office, but the looks and smirks they got from passing colleagues swiftly cured him of this ridiculous notion. He hoped that his red face would be attributed to the hot weather, although by now the mercury had dropped to a very pleasant twenty degrees.

Calderwood was waiting for them in McCord's office. Seeing Amy clinging to his boss's arm, he shot up from his chair.

"Amy, are you alright?"

"She's fine," McCord said. "Silly footwear. Has Palmer-Wycliffe arrived?"

"He's waiting in Interview Room 2," Calderwood said.

"Well then," McCord said, turning to go.

"What about me?" Amy complained. "You can't just leave me here!"

"Oh yes, we can," McCord said, already at the door. "We've got proper police work to do."

Amy was still muttering curses when the graceful figure of PC Dharwan entered the office, carrying a bottle of water and a first-aid box. "I saw you coming in and thought you could do with a drink."

Amy gratefully accepted.

"That must be sore," Dharwan said, pointing to Amy's ankles and handing her a box of paracetamol.

To her great annoyance, Amy felt herself welling up. McCord's rudeness she could cope with, but Dharwan's kindness was too much to bear. "It is." She sniffed and swallowed a couple of tablets.

"Put your feet up on the chair."

Dharwan bent down, poured some of the water on a tissue and wiped off the dried blood around the huge, angry-looking blisters that had turned into open wounds. Then she opened the box, disinfected the area around them and expertly applied a bandage.

"There," she said, "that should give you some relief."

"Thank you so much, Surina."

Amy was dying to ask her how her romance with Calderwood was coming along but Surina Dharwan had a natural dignity that made her disinclined to gossip. Still, Amy decided to put out some feelers.

"It's great that Duncan is back, isn't it?" she asked.

"Yes," Dharwan said. "He had a tough time after the shooting but thank God he has fully recovered. He was very brave."

Dharwan was not to be drawn any further but by her standards, Amy guessed, this amounted to a declaration of never-ending love.

"That is wonderful," Amy said, covering all angles of the situation. "How is the investigation going?"

Dharwan smiled. "You'd better ask the boss. I need to get back to work. Are you staying?"

Amy shook her head.

"There's no point sitting around here like a lemon. I'll get my mum to pick me up." And later, she would phone Calderwood to get the low-down on Palmer-Wycliffe.

* * *

In Interview Room 2, McCord and Calderwood were awaited by a much less ebullient Palmer-Wycliffe than before. His pallid complexion bore a striking similarity to that of his partner in crime, and McCord was keen to find out how much persuasion it would take to get him to put Morton Fisher's head on the block.

"Good evening, Mr Palmer-Wycliffe," McCord greeted him with grim cheerfulness. "I hear you have come to revise your statement?"

Palmer-Wycliffe rubbed his sweaty hands on another expensive tailor-made suit, while Calderwood switched on the recorder and stated date, time and the names of the people present.

"Yes, there is something I forgot to mention..." His voice trailed off.

McCord exchanged a grin with Calderwood. "I thought there might be. Please go ahead, Mr Palmer-Wycliffe, we're all ears."

"I should have told you before, but I was afraid..."

"There is no need to be afraid." Calderwood easily slid into the good cop, bad cop routine that he and McCord had perfected. "We can protect you against anybody who might be threatening you, and I can assure you that cooperation with the police is always regarded favourably."

Rather than encouraging Palmer-Wycliffe, Calderwood's words seemed to throw him, and he said nothing for a minute while staring at the chipped Formica tabletop in front of him.

McCord exchanged a glance with Calderwood and took over again. "Go on, tell us why you came here and be done with it," he said.

Palmer-Wycliffe looked up but shied away from the shrewd dark eyes that bored into him and addressed Calderwood instead.

"I was there, I mean, I was at Roseburn House when it was on fire, but I didn't burn it down!"

McCord was disappointed. While it was good to have Palmer-Wycliffe confirm what Chloe Chalmers had said, McCord really wanted something on Morton Fisher.

"Why don't you tell us from the beginning what happened that day," Calderwood suggested gently.

"I was on my parents' estate at Cedarfield House which is out on Lanark Road West a few miles past Balerno. I was worried about Vic–"

"I don't think so," McCord interrupted. "You had broken up with her the day before, which, incidentally, you also failed to mention at our last chat."

To his great satisfaction, he saw Palmer-Wycliffe blanch and pressed home his advantage.

"We know that you broke up with Ms Norval because we were able to retrieve some files from her phone."

Calderwood shot McCord a warning glance.

"Not much there," McCord said quickly, "but enough to prove that Ms Norval was deeply in love with you and very upset about the break-up. Could you enlighten us why you broke up with her?"

Palmer-Wycliffe was sweating profusely.

"It was because of Vic's post on Twitter. Before that, she wanted our affair kept secret because of her husband, but then suddenly she decided to tell the whole world about us. She never gave my feelings about it a second thought."

"She was in love," Calderwood said. "And she assumed that you loved her, too."

"So, what were your feelings that she so callously ignored?" McCord asked.

"I needed the relationship to remain a secret just as much as she did," Palmer-Wycliffe said, "because my parents would have been very upset if they had found out about our affair. My father is an elder in the Church of Scotland. He has very... old-fashioned ideas about relationships."

"You're a grown man," McCord said. "Why are you so afraid of what your father thinks?"

Palmer-Wycliffe pressed his lips together.

"We can always ask him ourselves, Mr Palmer-Wycliffe."

Palmer-Wycliffe almost jumped from his seat. "Please don't," he pleaded. "He has threatened to disinherit me unless I conduct myself in an… how shall I put it…"

"Honourable way?" McCord prompted. "I can imagine that you find that a difficult thing to do."

"I thought I was in love with her, but…"

McCord smiled grimly. "But when it came to the crunch, the money was more important, wasn't it? So, you broke up with her, but she wouldn't go quietly. She threatened to… what? Tell your father? You couldn't let that happen, so you drove to Edinburgh to shut her up permanently?"

"No!" Palmer-Wycliffe shouted. "That's exactly why I didn't tell you before because I knew you would think that. I had tried to contact her all day, but she didn't pick up. Then she phoned me. I had the impression she was very drunk. She said she was fed up with her life, and that Morton and I would be sorry. I went to Roseburn House because I thought she was going to kill herself. She sounded desperate on the phone. I hoped she might calm down if I managed to speak to her face to face. But I was too late. When I arrived, the house was on fire, and somehow, I knew she was in there. I could do nothing but watch." He buried his face in his hands.

McCord, chewing his lip, watched him dispassionately. He didn't believe a word Palmer-Wycliffe had said, but the arrogant sod had made a clever move. He'd come up with a plausible scenario for his presence at Roseburn House and pre-empted their accusation of obstructing a murder inquiry. And while Detective Chief Inspector bloody Baxter was bumbling around in his drugs investigation, McCord could not use the photos of the money drop as leverage to get a confession.

It was Calderwood's calm voice that brought him back to the interview.

"When did you leave your parents' estate?"

"I... I don't know, some time after half past six?" Palmer-Wycliffe stammered.

Calderwood pushed a piece of paper towards Palmer-Wycliffe.

"Please write down the address of Cedarfield House and your parents' contact details. We need to talk to them."

Palmer-Wycliffe hesitated and turned on his charm. "Do they need to know about all this, Inspector? Vic and me, I mean?"

McCord suspected that in the great scheme of things, Palmer-Wycliffe's affair with a married woman would be the least of his parents' worries.

Before he could say anything, however, Calderwood spoke up. "We'll have to confirm the timings. If you had been straight with us from the start, all this would not have been necessary at all."

Palmer-Wycliffe made a contrite face. "I do realise that. I'm very sorry."

You will be, McCord thought. "Do you believe that Morton Fisher killed his wife?" he asked.

Palmer-Wycliffe shrugged. "I have no idea. If he was the jealous type, maybe he could have done it."

McCord signalled to Calderwood to end the recording.

"You can go for now, Mr Palmer-Wycliffe. But we are going to meet again soon, no doubt."

Chapter 13

The following morning found Amy sitting at one of the few tables outside Loudons, a charming café situated most conveniently right opposite the offices of the Financial Conduct Authority in Fountainbridge. After a great deal of humming and hawing, Duncan Calderwood had provided her with Stuart McLellan's work and home addresses on the condition that she would not, under any circumstances, approach him on her own, which she had solemnly promised.

The warm spell continued, and Amy enjoyed wearing yet another summer dress albeit with moccasins whose soft leather mostly hid the thick plaster covering the shrinking blisters on her ankles. She had been here since eleven thirty hoping to catch Stuart McLellan going out for lunch. There was no picture of the employees on the FCA website, but Amy had found a Facebook post on Danielle McLellan's account from several years ago, taken in happier times and showing her with her husband and a baby gawping quizzically at the camera. Apparently even then, Hunter had been full of questions.

Amy had to agree with Patrick Fisher, though. In that picture, Stuart McLellan was oddly lacking in any distinguishing features, and Amy worried that she might not recognise him when he left the building. She was not sure what she was hoping to find out; it was unlikely, after all, that he should assault anybody during his lunch hour, but she wanted to gain her own impression of the man she suspected to be a control freak and a sadist.

Amy was on her second latte when someone exited the FCA offices, crossed the road and walked towards her. It was a slightly older version of the man she had seen on Facebook, dressed in a cheap grey suit which made him even more indistinct, like an insect hiding in plain sight.

For an anxious moment, Amy wondered if he knew who she was and why she was here. Was he coming over to confront her? But he simply entered the outdoor area through a small metal gate and headed for the table next to her that was being vacated as he approached.

He had barely sat down when he took out his phone and called a number on speed dial. As it kept ringing, he became more and more agitated.

"Yes!" he barked at the waiter who had approached the table asking if he wanted lunch. "The soup and tap water, and a black coffee afterwards. And hurry, I need to get back to work."

Makes sense, Amy thought. The grey man ordering the only two boring items on the menu.

The waiter withdrew with a sour face and Amy wondered if McLellan's soup would come enriched with a healthy blob of spit.

McLellan, meanwhile, was attempting to make another call. "Pick up, you useless bitch," Amy heard him hiss under his breath.

McLellan suddenly looked up. Even his eyes were grey. "What are you staring at?" he snarled at her.

"Nothing, sorry," Amy said, quickly regaining her composure. "It sounded as if you were in trouble. Can I help you at all?"

"Mind your own business," came the answer.

Amy demonstratively focused on her latte, annoyed with herself. It was a rookie mistake to draw attention to yourself while observing a suspect.

The waiter appeared and put McLellan's soup and water in front of him without a smile. Then he turned to Amy.

"Would you like to order some lunch?"

Amy saw that a small queue had formed at the door and the people waiting were longingly eyeing up the seats outside, hoping for spaces to become available.

"Could I possibly have some buttered toast?" Amy asked with her most dazzling smile. "I won't have time for a full lunch, unfortunately."

The waiter withdrew with a slight bow. Amy pretended to look at her phone but could not resist peeking across to McLellan who was tapping furiously on his screen. He must be mad at Danielle for taking herself and Hunter off to a place where he could not get at her. Or at *them*? Amy began to wonder what Hunter had seen or suffered at home. He did not display the characteristics of an abused child, but one never knew. Children were incredibly resilient, but also very good at hiding their fear and pain. She decided she would have to try to get him on his own and speak to him. But at The Braemar, Patrick Fisher would at best ignore her, and Danielle McLellan had not been enthused by her attempts to help either.

The waiter returned with her toast. She nibbled on it until McLellan had finished his soup and toasted focaccia, downed his coffee and disappeared back into the office building.

No, there was nothing for it, she would have to stay on Stuart McLellan's tail.

* * *

Amy was not sure when McLellan would finish work, but Loudons closed at three o'clock, so she had decided to go home for a while and then hang around in front of the student halls just down the road from the FCA. After her previous encounter with McLellan, she had thought it wise to use a disguise, and had dug out a pair of torn jeans, an old T-shirt and trainers she had used during the Rock Killer case. Her long, black hair was hidden under a cap emblazoned with a saltire that she had bought on a whim some time ago on the Royal Mile after having imbibed a few too many. A pair of cheap sunglasses that hid most of her face completed the disguise. It was a good job that her mother wasn't here to see this. Valerie, a sewing lady turned successful fashion designer, would never have stood for her daughter being dressed like a tramp, and the mere idea of her shadowing a potentially violent man on her own would have sent her into a fit. That was why Amy had also kept her outing a secret from John, who was almost as much of a mother hen as Valerie, as well as a hopeless liar.

Why is it that everybody thinks I'm that fragile little thing, she thought angrily. Not that she didn't like being attractive, but there was more to her than that, and she was going to prove it to them, her mum and John, and most of all, to DI McCord.

As she wandered up and down the pavement, she noticed to her dismay that most of the students were far better dressed than she was, and not one of them was wearing a cap as naff as hers.

Her musings were interrupted by McLellan stepping out into the street and purposefully striding in the direction of Haymarket. Amy gave him a head start and then followed him cautiously, her phone ready to pretend she was texting somebody. McLellan never turned round, though, and to Amy's surprise, he walked past the station along West Coates towards the Water of Leith. Amy could not believe her luck. He was going to The Braemar, no doubt to claim back his family. Maybe he'd create a scene and would be arrested? Then his abusive behaviour would be revealed, and Danielle would be safe; she'd make sure of that.

On her way, it occurred to Amy that McLellan had another reason to want his wife back. Morton Fisher's daughter stood to inherit a tidy sum of money on her father's death. Maybe that had been his intention all along, to marry the golden goose, but his attempt to exert total control over her had finally backfired. It was Amy's mission to liberate Danielle from the brutal prison she had been living in. And, of course, this would make a splendid article for the magazine.

* * *

As McLellan was walking along Corstorphine Road and eventually reached The Braemar's driveway, Amy was conscious that her disguise was not ideal; most people around here were donning designer clothes and expensive shoes, and with McLellan hovering by the gate instead of entering the grounds, she risked being noticed by him. Thankfully, the owners of the property next door had prioritised practicality over aesthetics and placed a sizeable shed next to their gate, leaving a neat space behind it for Amy to hide and observe what was going on outside The Braemar.

McLellan was tapping angrily on his phone again, and not getting the desired answer, he made his way up the drive. Amy climbed onto an upturned bucket to be able to peek over the wall.

McLellan was being met by a waiter whose body language suggested that he was asking him politely to leave. McLellan shouted at the waiter that he had every right to be here and see his wife and son. The answer must have been negative because McLellan began to swear profusely.

To Amy's astonishment, she heard a familiar voice. She stretched to see Hunter coming down the drive.

Always keeping well behind the waiter, he was now addressing his father.

"Leave us alone," he shouted. "I know what you've been doing to Mum. Go away!"

The anger in McLellan's voice turned to anxiety.

"Hunter, son, don't listen to her! She's lying! She is mentally unstable!"

"No, *you* are lying," Hunter shouted, choking away tears. "I saw what you did to her, remember?"

"You misunderstood the situation," McLellan pleaded. "Sometimes adults... do things that are frightening to children because they don't understand."

"I know what I saw; I'm not stupid," Hunter said, tears running down his face. "Leave us alone!"

"I really must ask you to go now, sir," the waiter said to McLellan, "or I'll have to call the police."

Amy ducked as McLellan spun round and reappeared on the road, cursing Danielle as well as the waiter. He paced up and down until he had reached a decision. Walking swiftly, he started to head back into the city.

Amy followed McLellan back to Haymarket where he disappeared into a pub. Thinking that he might be in there for a while, she decided to go in as well. She gave it a minute, then she pushed the heavy door open. McLellan was leaning with his back to the bar, waiting for the barman to pull him a pint. He was looking straight at her. Had he spotted her after all on his way here? Amy hesitated for a fraction of a second. If he saw her outside again, waiting for him, it would seem even more suspicious. Avoiding his gaze, she went up to the bar and ordered a tonic water. As soon as she had done that, she knew she had made another mistake. Somebody dressed like her was much more likely to order a Coke or some other abomination. As she swiped her card, she saw out of the corner of her eye McLellan carrying his Newcastle Brown Ale and a chaser to a table in the back corner. Picking up her drink, she moved along the bar until she was out of his sight.

After a few minutes she had finished her drink and stretched over to see him deep in thought nursing his pint. When one of the punters left, McLellan did not even look up.

Heeding her mother's advice to be always ready for the unexpected – although Valerie had most certainly not anticipated a scenario such as this – Amy had come prepared, and now she was glad she had. She sneaked into the Ladies and exchanged her crummy outfit for a jersey wraparound dress and the cap for a painted scarf. It caused her physical pain having to wear trainers with the elegant dress, but another pair of shoes had not fitted into her bag, and sandals were out of the question. Well, one had to make sacrifices. She fervently hoped that McLellan was not too observant.

A small table had become vacant while she was away, so she put her bag on one of the seats and ordered a glass of white wine. The barman showed no sign of recognition. I'm getting better at this, she thought.

McLellan ordered another three pints and chasers over the next hour and a half while Amy was trying to make her second glass of sauvignon blanc last as long as possible. She was beginning to think that McLellan was going to spend all night here to get blind drunk. She was about to give up on her surveillance mission when he suddenly got up and left. Hurriedly, she grabbed her bag, but it slipped and spilled the contents all over the floor. A portly man, who ogled her cleavage as she bent down, got up from his seat. Curtly rejecting his offer to help, she stuffed the manky clothes into the bag and rushed outside.

McLellan was nowhere to be seen.

Muttering an oath, Amy turned towards the station. To her immense relief, she spotted McLellan at the top of the taxi rank. He was exchanging a few words with the driver.

Without hesitating a moment, Amy climbed into the taxi behind.

"Follow the cab in front but keep a discreet distance, please."

The driver, a middle-aged, cloth-capped Edinburgh man, grinned.

"Your man cheating on you?" he asked as he pulled away from the kerb.

Amy gave no reply, even though this confirmed the driver's suspicion. He waited for the taxi in front to join the lane and after letting a few cars pass, he squeezed into the same line of traffic. The roads were quieter now that the rush hour was over, and the revellers had not come out yet. The driver regarded Amy in the back mirror with open curiosity.

"Don't you worry, ma'am, I'll stay on him."

It was past seven o'clock but still broad daylight outside. McLellan's taxi, with Amy's not far behind, meandered through the streets from Haymarket, along Shandwick Place and down Stafford Street. When they turned right onto Melville Street, Amy's heart sank. McLellan must be heading home to his flat on Randolph Crescent. But then the taxi in front continued on its way. Where on earth was McLellan heading? Finally, his taxi stopped on Hamilton Place.

Amy's driver reacted fast. In a move worthy of a Formula One race, he slammed on the brakes and pulled into a tight spot behind a lorry, which shielded them from sight.

About twenty yards in front, McLellan alighted and unsteadily crossed the road into Clarence Street. Amy thanked her driver and handed him a ten-pound note as she stepped onto the pavement.

"I don't think you should follow him, dear," said the driver. "I know this area and I have a fair idea where he's going. A lovely young lady like you can do better than chase after a drunken sleazebag! Why don't you let me take you home?"

Amy smiled and shook her head. "No, thanks."

With a regretful wave, he drove off.

Amy had never been in this part of Stockbridge before but something about the name seemed familiar. And then she remembered. A couple of years ago, this area had been notorious for the operations of the infamous Archie Turnbull who was now, with a little help from McCord, safely behind bars.

Chapter 14

Amy watched as McLellan eventually stopped at a crumbling Victorian building, rang the bell and waited, tapping his foot impatiently. After a little while, he was admitted. When the door had closed behind him, Amy cautiously approached the entrance. A scuffed, formerly shiny sign above proclaimed it to be The Orchard, and underneath, a rusty metal sign read 'Welcome'.

Amy waited for a while wondering what kind of business was operating here, and if it was perhaps part of an FCA investigation. But then, surely, McLellan would not have drunk so much. She had no desire to hang around this dingy place until McLellan was finished, but some instinct told her to wait.

Amy crossed the road and replied to her emails to pass the time.

She was about to press the send button for the third time, when there was a commotion at the entrance of The Orchard. Amy slunk into the shadow of the nearest doorway. A burly man had McLellan by the collar and was depositing him unceremoniously on the pavement before returning into the building. McLellan smoothed down his shirt and tucked it into the grey suit. He was not wearing a tie anymore. Pretending not to notice the stares and guffaws from the small crowd that had quickly formed to watch the spectacle, McLellan walked stiffly away in the direction of Hamilton Place. He had obviously decided to head for home.

This place has absolutely nothing to do with the FCA and John would not like this at all, Amy thought. Her mum would also strongly disapprove if she could see what Amy was about to do, but her nose told her to do an interview of a different kind, and they were not here to see it.

She waited for the onlookers to disperse before she crossed the road and pressed the bell. The heavy, wooden door of The Orchard opened with a buzz, and she found herself in a hallway guarded by the burly man she had seen a few minutes before. His tight-fitting black T-shirt stretched across his six-pack and bulging biceps. He had the short neck of a bulldog and eyes that stood too close together in a pockmarked face.

Amy swallowed. "Hi," she said, far too cheerfully.

The bouncer looked at her with surprise.

"I don't think this is your kind of scene, hen," he said, scanning her up and down with a frown. "Unless you're hard-up and needing work?"

Amy could see behind him a heavily made-up woman who was dressed in very little but a flimsy dressing gown and who eyed her curiously.

Finally realising what kind of business this was, Amy blushed and shook her head. "I'm interested in that man you threw out just now. What's he done?"

The bouncer's expression became more guarded.

"You his wife or what?" he asked.

Amy snorted. "Not likely. I'm from *Forth Write* magazine."

"From the press? Dolly won't like this at all. You'd better leave."

"Is Dolly the... manager? Could I please speak to her?" Amy asked. "I'm investigating a criminal case, and it might be advantageous to Dolly to cooperate. Why don't you let her decide?"

The bouncer was sceptical. "Wait here," he said, but then he had second thoughts. "No, you'd better come with me. You'll scare off the punters standing there like that."

"Oh, thanks very much," Amy said, pretending to be in a huff. "If I'd known, I'd have worn a miniskirt and a bra with tassels."

The bouncer's face transformed as he laughed. "I didn't mean it like that, miss."

"I know," Amy said, breaking into a laugh too.

He led the way past a half-circular stairwell into a time warp. Amy entered a Victorian lounge cluttered with heavy wooden sofas and armchairs covered in threadbare red velvet. Dusty embroidered curtains that were worn thin where they had been pulled for decades kept out every ray of sunshine. Instead, the room was lit by little curved lamps emanating a soft, dim light that flattered the employees as well as the clients, Amy suspected. In the back corner there was a bar. The woman in the dressing gown had gone; there was nobody to be seen.

"Not exactly heaving, is it?" Amy asked as the bouncer walked across the lounge towards a room at the far end.

"Still early. The place only livens up after ten." At the door, he hesitated. "Dolly won't like this one bit," he said again, knocking gently three times.

By now, Amy had become quite apprehensive about this Dolly character.

"Come in!" shouted a rasping voice from within, and the bouncer opened the door.

His bulk filled the frame, so Amy could not see beyond him.

"There's a young lady here to see you, boss. She says she's from" – he turned round to check with Amy – "*Forth Write* magazine."

"*Forth Write* magazine?" the voice croaked. "How exciting. Show her in, Jimmy, don't be so rude!" A giggle, cut short by a fit of coughing, greeted Amy as Jimmy stepped aside to let her in.

"Thank you, Jimmy, you can go back to your duties. If you're needed for an interview, I'll call you." Another giggle and a cough.

What Amy now faced, she had not expected. A woman suitably dressed for a ladies' afternoon tea stood in the middle of a small, shabby office dominated by a huge rubber plant. The air of respectability created by the coiffed waves and the elegant two-piece and discreet pearl necklace, however, was seriously undermined by the yellow-stained teeth clamped around a cigar that was hanging out of the corner of the woman's mouth.

Amy shook a very firm hand.

"Hi, I'm Dolly. And you must be Amy Thornton, am I right?"

Amy was astounded. "You've read my articles?"

"Just because I run a brothel, it doesn't mean I'm illiterate," Dolly said with a slight irritation in her voice. "But don't flatter yourself, I only enjoy reading the ones about your shenanigans with DI McCord. You haven't done those for a while, so I stopped buying the magazine. What happened, have you two fallen out or something?"

Amy ignored the question. Something else interested her much more. "You know DI McCord?"

Another laugh caused a degree of breathlessness that began to alarm Amy. But she knew better than to point out to smokers the causal relationship between their habit and lung cancer.

"McCord and I go back a long way," Dolly gasped. "And he's always been good to my girls, especially Candy."

McCord and Dolly? Go back a long way? And good to Candy? What? She thought back to the awkward hug they had shared during the Rock Killer case and the dance at the charity ball; his warm hand on her back and his breath caressing her hair; the look on his face when he woke up in hospital and saw her there; McCord, who had thrown himself into the path of a bullet, frequenting a brothel? She suddenly realised how little she knew about the man with whom she had solved four murder cases. She had never been to his home. They had never talked, or rather quarrelled, about anything but the cases they were involved in. What else was there? Was he secretly married or had a love child – with a prostitute?! It would certainly explain his awkwardness around her…

She was vaguely aware of Dolly saying something. "Pardon?"

"I asked you why you wanted to speak to me." The corners of Dolly's mouth twitched. "Was it about the creep I had thrown out earlier?"

Amy was desperate to question Dolly about McCord, but it was simply too humiliating, so she forced herself back to her mission.

"Yes, he's called Stuart McLellan. What did he do?"

"He swore at one of my girls, slapped her, and when he began to use his fists, she pressed the alarm button. Jimmy sorted him out. I don't think he'll be back."

"Would she testify to that in court?" Amy asked excitedly.

"Of course not," Dolly said, "don't be silly. Who believes a working girl when it's her word against a 'respectable' citizen's? We need to look after ourselves. Nobody else does. Except maybe McCord."

There he was again, the hero of the whorehouse.

Suddenly, she did not want to hear any more.

"Thank you for talking to me," Amy said.

At the door, she turned round. "Do you really have alarm buttons in the rooms?"

"Of course! I do take care of my girls, you know."

* * *

Outside, the long dusk had begun to obscure the shabbiness of the street with a soft haze. She needed to speak to somebody about the revelations concerning McCord's private life. Her mum? Good God, no. John? He would squirm at the mere mention of prostitution and be unable to imagine McCord being involved in anything so sordid. Martin? He thought the world of McCord and would make a terrible scene. Duncan Calderwood? He was most likely to know but he was fiercely loyal to McCord and probably would not tell her even if he knew. As she went through the list of the people she was closest to, it did not occur to her for a second that the person she ought to ask was McCord himself.

Chapter 15

On Monday morning, Gilchrist called McCord into his office. As always when a member of the upper echelons of society was in McCord's sights, the superintendent was in a state of heightened anxiety mixed with fury.

"Is there any particular reason why you keep bothering James Palmer-Wycliffe? His mother has been complaining to my wife during their book club meetings that he is worried sick, and when she insisted on knowing why, he told her that the police seem to have it in for him and keep pestering him about this house fire he was allegedly at. You don't seriously think that the son of the Palmer-Wycliffes would burn down a five-million-pound mansion? Is there anything at all my wife can tell his mother to give her peace of mind?"

"Afraid not, sir," McCord said, unmoved by the rant. "The only reason that James Palmer-Wycliffe has not been arrested yet for complicity in money laundering, is because the drug squad is gathering more evidence against him and the other members of the gang for whom he has been working. We have a witness placing him at the fire which killed Victoria Norval, who had threatened to expose their affair, and probably also his criminal activities. I'd suggest the less your wife says to Mrs Palmer-Wycliffe over the next few days, the better. In fact, it might be wise for Mrs Gilchrist to avoid any contact with the family altogether until this investigation is concluded."

Gilchrist's mouth hung open for a couple of seconds before he had grasped the enormity of the situation.

"Good Lord!" he whispered.

"We don't have irrefutable proof where the murder by arson charge is concerned," McCord admitted. "DS Calderwood and I have just been to the parents' estate out past Balerno to check the exact time when he left that afternoon. Of course, they are not the most reliable witnesses where their dear son is concerned, but we needed to take their statements and those of their employees anyway. Timings are tight, but if he broke the speed limit, he could have made it in time to set the fire. We'll need to check the Lanark Road traffic cameras on the route he would have taken to be sure."

Gilchrist closed his eyes at the thought of McCord conducting the interview with the Palmer-Wycliffes like a rhinoceros trampling across a field of delicate flowers.

"I trust you let DS Calderwood handle this one?" he asked with a glimmer of hope in his eyes.

McCord was not about to tell him that he had.

"I shall next time, sir," McCord said and left the office with a grin.

* * *

Back in his Sunset Boulevard, McCord found Amy chatting to Calderwood.

"Miss Thornton," he said with mock surprise, "how are you getting on with your domestic abuse case?"

"Very well, as a matter of fact," she said.

He was taken aback by the coldness in her voice. They had squabbled, of course, last time they met, but didn't they always? She also seemed to scrutinise his face, and he wondered if he had an ink mark on his nose or something stuck between his teeth. Furtively, he sent his tongue on an exploratory wander but could not feel anything untoward.

"It's obvious to me that you are not interested in what I have to say," Amy continued angrily, "but I'll tell you anyway. I think you should be investigating Stuart McLellan."

McCord, of course, loved it when she told him what and whom to investigate.

"And why should we do that?" he said, annoyed now himself.

"Because he is a seriously nasty character. I believe that he is abusing Danielle and trying to control her because he is after her money and future inheritance. After work on Friday, he went to The Braemar to get hold of her, but they would not let him in. Hunter came out and basically told him he knew what he did to his mum and to leave them alone."

"Good for him," McCord said. "Very brave, doing that."

"And after that," Amy continued, "McLellan went to The Orchard, but he was thrown out of the building for assaulting one of the girls."

"What is The Orchard?" Calderwood interrupted.

"It's a brothel," Amy said, again fixing her gaze on McCord, who was getting concerned now.

"I'd rather you didn't go anywhere near The Orchard," McCord said. "Not the best part of town for a woman to go for an evening stroll on her own."

"You'd be the expert on that, of course," Amy said, pausing for effect. "I had a nice chat with Dolly, by the way, and she sends her love."

"Who is Dolly?" Calderwood asked, increasingly confused by the turn the conversation had taken.

"Dolly is the owner and manager of this entirely legal establishment," McCord explained. "A woman not to be crossed, but she has a heart of gold. Great banter too, especially after a couple of Bell's. A couple of glasses, that is." McCord laughed at the memory.

"Right," Calderwood said, exchanging a glance with Amy.

McCord had noticed. "Look at you two snobs turning up your noses. Can I remind you that we are in the middle of a murder investigation? Amy, by all means, take your case to the Domestic Abuse Investigation Officer or Women's Aid, but we are homicide detectives. If we chased every misogynistic thug in the city, we'd never be done. And anyway, Danielle has left her husband and gone to live with her father, hasn't she?"

"That husband of hers won't give up so easily," Amy said. "But fine, why don't we all wait until she's found dead in a ditch somewhere, and then you two can jump into action and figure out who it was. That is policing at its very best."

Amy yanked her handbag from the back of the chair and stormed out of the office.

McCord turned to Calderwood. "What's wrong with her? Can she not see that domestics are not in our remit?"

"To be fair, it does sound serious," Calderwood said. "I think she is worried that Danielle, and maybe even Hunter, are in danger."

McCord contemplated this. "It's possible, I suppose. We could have a wee word with Mr McLellan, so he is aware that we are keeping an eye on him. That should do it, don't you think?"

Calderwood sighed.

"What's wrong now?" McCord asked, drumming his fingers on the desktop.

"I was wondering, sir, why you didn't say that to Amy. She doesn't feel that she is being taken seriously. And then that whole brothel thing!"

"What brothel thing?" McCord asked, perplexed.

Calderwood hesitated.

"Come on, spit it out!"

"Well" – Calderwood struggled to find the right words – "obviously, she was not thrilled to find out that you are… visiting brothels."

"Visiting…?" McCord was speechless for a moment. "Who says I'm visiting brothels? I met Dolly as a DC when some clever clogs high up in the force thought they could root out prostitution in the city by prosecuting the women who are trapped in that life. Dolly was one of those who ran a clean establishment, paid her girls well and looked after them. No drugs, no coercion, nobody underage. Since then, I've checked up on the place occasionally, and she keeps me up to date with what's going on in the area. And in the McAdie case – last year, before you joined – one of her girls helped me find a mole in our own department here at St Leonard's. Dolly's been a very useful contact."

He paused to catch his breath and looked at Calderwood, wide-eyed. "Let me get this straight. You're suggesting that Amy thinks that I'm…?"

"Sleeping with prostitutes, yes," Calderwood clarified it for him. "And she doesn't like it, and not because she's a snob."

McCord had not listened to the last part of the sentence.

"How can she possibly think that of me?" he said indignantly. "After all that we…"

Then an idea occurred to him. "I wonder if Dolly has been up to mischief. I wouldn't put it past her. I must ask her what she said to Amy."

Calderwood sighed again. "Don't you think you should speak to Amy instead, sir?"

"Why should I? If she has such a low opinion of me, there's not much point, is there?" McCord said angrily. "Before we know it, on the say-so of some lowlife, she'll believe I'm part of a paedophile ring. It's just hopeless."

"Sometimes I fear that it is," Calderwood said, shaking his head, "absolutely hopeless."

McCord was about to say something when the phone rang. He listened intently, his face changing from incredulity to resignation.

"Alright," he said, "we're on our way."

"What's happened?" Calderwood asked.

"Morton Fisher is dead."

Chapter 16

The genteel calm of The Braemar was shattered by flashing blue lights and people in white overalls purposefully going about their business in the back garden. Curious onlookers were kept at bay by blue-and-white crime-scene tape stretched across the entry to the drive, watched over by a bored PC.

On McCord's instructions, the guests had all been kept inside. The early afternoon sun was beating down mercilessly on the wilting flowers and yellowing grass as McCord and Calderwood made their way towards the pond that was sheltered from the sun by surrounding trees. The earthly remains of Morton Fisher were splayed by the side of the pool, his head face down in the water.

Kneeling next to the body was the squat figure of Dr Crane.

"Good afternoon, DI McCord. Quite interesting, this one. There is slight bruising on the back of the neck, indicating that somebody pushed his head down but there are no signs of a struggle. I'll need to have a closer look when I've got him on the table. Fancy coming along to watch?" he asked with a grin.

"No, thanks," McCord said. "Any idea when he died?"

"An hour ago, or an hour and a half at the most, I'd say. It'll all be in my PM."

"Great. Tomorrow?"

"It's all take and no give with you, DI McCord. But tomorrow it is."

Crane got up to make room for the ambulance drivers who would take the body to the morgue. As they began to shift the body onto its back and then a stretcher, McCord turned away. Even if he had heartily disliked the man when he was alive, he had no desire to see his terror-stricken face in death.

"Come on, Calderwood, let's hear what the relatives have to say."

* * *

The main door was being guarded by a young, female PC who seemed rather excited. Maybe it was her first murder. Seeing McCord and Calderwood, both of whom had become celebrities during their last case together and were regarded with something akin to awe by their colleagues, she was positively enraptured.

"So pleased to meet you, DI McCord, DS Calderwood," she stammered and ran her fingers through her spiky black hair.

"And you are?" McCord asked kindly.

"PC McGlashan, sir."

"How are things inside?"

"Everybody is shocked, sir, as you can imagine," she said. "Especially the poor lad."

McCord had difficulty picturing Hunter as a 'poor lad'.

"I didn't have the impression that he was very close to his grandfather," he said.

"Maybe not," McGlashan said, "but it was him who found the body."

"Good God, that is terrible. But knowing Hunter, he'll have the mystery solved for us in no time. Where is he?"

"In his mother's room, number twenty-one; his uncle is in there with them."

"Thank you, PC McGlashan."

As they walked up the broad, carpeted stairs, McCord said, "I'd really like to speak to Hunter on his own, but I suppose with him being a child, there has to be an adult there as well. In any case, we need to interview Patrick Fisher. Call Turner and Dharwan; I want my people here to take statements from the staff and the other guests."

Calderwood made the call, while McCord knocked firmly on door number twenty-one.

"Come in," a shaky voice sounded from inside.

Danielle McLellan was sitting on the bed, propped up by several cushions, her arms wrapped tightly around her son whose face was buried in her shoulder. Her hair was dishevelled, and her eyes were red and swollen. Patrick Fisher rose from the armchair he was sitting in and solemnly accepted the detectives' condolences. McCord thought that he was very composed considering his father had been found dead not two hours ago.

"We'd like a word with your sister and nephew first," McCord said. "We'll speak to you afterwards in your room."

Patrick Fisher hesitated. "Are you going to be alright?" he asked Danielle but looked at Hunter.

"We'll be fine," Danielle said, although it did not sound convincing. "See you later."

After Patrick had left, Calderwood pulled up the chair that stood in front of the dressing table while McCord lowered himself into the armchair. He did not like sitting so low nor leaning back, so he shifted position until he was perched forward on the edge of the seat.

"Hunter, my favourite assistant detective," he said brightly, "are you up to answering a few questions?"

Hunter turned his tear-streaked face towards the detectives but remained in the foetal position he had adopted. McCord suddenly realised that Hunter was still just a little boy, obviously traumatised by the events.

"Can you tell us what happened?" McCord asked, quietly now.

Hunter wiped his nose with the back of his hand.

"After lunch, I went out to play in the garden, and when I got to the pond, I found Grandpa lying there with his face in the water." Hunter began to sob. "I know I should have checked his pulse, but I didn't want to touch him. He didn't move at all, so I ran back to the hotel and got help."

"That was exactly the right thing to do," Calderwood reassured the boy.

"Did you see anybody around there at that time or notice anything strange?" McCord asked hopefully.

Hunter shook his head and hid his face again.

Trying not to let his disappointment show, McCord addressed Danielle McLellan.

"When did you last see your father?"

"Briefly, in the lobby, at around ten. He'd had breakfast before us. We wondered why he didn't join us for lunch, but it was not that unusual. He often snacked during the day and had his main meal at dinner time."

She pulled out a tissue and blew her nose.

"What frame of mind was he in when you met him? Did anything unusual happen today?" McCord asked.

"When I saw him this morning, he was quite agitated. He had a letter in his hand, and I asked him what the matter was, but he wouldn't tell me. I wanted to speak to him, but..."

She started to cry.

Hunter lifted his head, pulled out his right arm and instead of being held, embraced his mother. "Please, don't, Mum," he whispered. Then he turned to McCord. "We went shopping after that and came back for lunch."

"And during lunch, you and your brother were together?" McCord asked Danielle McLellan.

"Yes, we usually have lunch together."

"I mean, did you both stay at the table the whole time or did either of you nip to the toilet or out for a smoke, for example?"

"I can't remember," Danielle said, suddenly flustered, "I don't know anything anymore..."

Hunter sat up straight.

"Uncle Patrick, Mum and I were at the table all the time," he said. "Apart from a few minutes when Uncle Patrick went to the toilet," he added reluctantly.

"How long was he away for?" McCord asked, leaning even further forward.

"It wasn't him!" Hunter shouted suddenly. "Leave him alone!"

"I'm sorry, Hunter, but I have to ask those questions," McCord said. "There are things a detective sometimes has to do that are not nice." He passed a picture of James Palmer-Wycliffe to them. "Did either of you see this man in or around the hotel today?"

Both shook their heads.

"And your husband, Mrs McLellan? Was he here today, by any chance?"

"No," Danielle McLellan said, "at least I don't think so. The staff here know not to let him into the hotel, but he could have been hanging around outside."

Calderwood had paused taking notes. "Have you considered reporting your husband to the police for abuse and stalking? We–"

"How do you know about that?" she interrupted him.

"Amy Thornton has spoken to us about you. She wants to help but we can do very little without a formal complaint," he said gently.

Danielle McLellan was pulling at the hems of her long sleeves. Tears were streaming down her face, and she kept shaking her head.

"There are people who can help," Calderwood insisted. "Please think about it."

Danielle McLellan lowered her head and wiped her face with a fresh tissue. "Maybe."

McCord rose. "If you remember anything else, however insignificant it may seem to you, please let us know." He placed his card on the dressing table. "I hope you feel better soon, Hunter. It's a horrible thing for anyone to have to deal with."

Hunter nodded. "Thanks."

"Are you sure it's murder?" Danielle McLellan asked. "Could it not have been an accident? My father did not look well this morning, and when I spoke to him, he said he had terrible heartburn."

"That seems to have been a frequent occurrence with him," McCord said. "He mentioned it to me as well. However, it's not a condition that usually kills people. We need to wait for the post-mortem, but there are clear indicators that this is a suspicious death, so for now we are treating it as such. Where is your brother's room?"

"Number twenty-two, right next door," she said. "But surely, you can't think that Patrick..."

"Routine inquiries, nothing to worry about," McCord answered her unspoken question.

"That's what they always say, Mum," Hunter piped up, "even if that person is their number one suspect."

Danielle looked alarmed, but both McCord and Calderwood could not suppress a grin. Hunter was going to be fine.

* * *

It took a while for Patrick Fisher to answer the knock on the door. He was pale, and when he sat down, he held his fingers intertwined but still did not manage to stop them from shaking.

Delayed shock, or the realisation that it isn't as easy as it used to be to get away with murder? McCord wondered.

Calderwood pulled out his notebook. "I am sorry I have to ask this, Mr Fisher, but can you account for your movements today before and during lunch until your father's body was found?"

Patrick Fisher fixed his gaze on the wall behind them as if trying to remember.

"After breakfast, I was working on my CV and read through some job adverts until I met my sister and Hunter in the restaurant for lunch."

McCord exchanged a look with Calderwood. 'Aye, right,' it said.

"My sister and I were still eating," Patrick Fisher continued, "when Hunter went out to play and... you know. The poor wee soul. My sister was adamant that he should stay until the end of the meal, but I said to let him go and enjoy the sunshine. I wish now I had kept my mouth shut and supported her, then he would have been with us and wouldn't be left forever with the picture of his dead grandfather in his head."

"Yes, that was unfortunate," McCord said coolly, "but it would have been better if your father had not been murdered in the first place."

Patrick Fisher frowned. "Obviously."

"Do you have any witnesses for the time you claim you were in your room?"

"Obviously not," Patrick Fisher said, and a hint of aggression had crept into his voice. "I was alone the whole time."

"And when you went to the toilet during lunch, did anybody see you?"

Patrick Fisher's face showed first surprise, then annoyance. "I don't know. The staff might have done. You'd have to ask them."

"Oh, we will, Mr Fisher," McCord said. "Please don't leave the hotel without notifying us."

And without any further formalities, McCord marched out of the door, while Calderwood politely bade Patrick Fisher goodbye.

* * *

"I'm surprised you didn't arrest him," Calderwood said when they stepped outside into the afternoon heat. "He had motive, means and opportunity."

"We have nothing solid on him yet, and I don't think he is going anywhere in a hurry. First, we need to get our hands on Palmer-Wycliffe," McCord said. "He has an even stronger motive. He knew we were putting pressure on Fisher and feared he was about to crack. I thought it was because Fisher had killed Norval, but what if Palmer-Wycliffe killed her and Fisher figured that out?"

"Morton Fisher would never have grassed on Palmer-Wycliffe, though," Calderwood said, "because then the whole money laundering story would have come out."

"Maybe," McCord said. "But murder is a completely different ball game, and Fisher knew that he was in the frame for it. He might have thought that we would offer him a deal for giving us Palmer-Wycliffe and the whole drugs operation with it, and he would have had no qualms about landing others in the mess to save his own skin. Palmer-Wycliffe had to get rid of Fisher to be sure he wouldn't talk. We'll pick him up right now before he charters a private plane and disappears."

"But what about the drug squad?" Calderwood asked. "They won't like it if we interfere with their operation."

“Tough,” McCord said. “But if you insist, I’ll give them a courtesy call.”

While McCord was waiting to be put through to DCI Baxter, he and Calderwood retreated into the shade of a flowering rowan tree. McCord sniffed the air. “Puh, what a stink.”

“I think the smell attracts beetles and flies,” Calderwood said.

“No wonder,” McCord said, “considering what they usually go for. Yes?” He held his phone closer to his ear. “DCI Baxter? I wanted to let you know that Morton Fisher has been found dead. First indications are that he was murdered. I’m on my way to arrest James Palmer-Wycliffe. I believe he poses a flight risk.”

“There’s no need to worry, DI McCord,” Baxter said in an infuriatingly slow drawl. “We arrested Palmer-Wycliffe and the whole gang a couple of hours ago.”

McCord felt the heat rising in his face.

“And it did not occur to you to inform me of that?”

“Last time I looked, I did not have to justify my actions to an officer of inferior rank,” Baxter said, sharply now. “If you want to talk to him, let me know and I’ll arrange a suitable time. At the moment, we are busy interviewing everybody. Goodbye, DI McCord.”

Thankfully, Baxter ended the call before McCord could tell him exactly how he felt.

Calderwood waited patiently until McCord had calmed down and related the conversation with Baxter. “Two hours?” He checked his watch. “That means Palmer-Wycliffe is off the hook, for Fisher’s murder at least.”

Chapter 17

Crane was as good as his word and emailed the post-mortem report first thing the following morning. After he had read it, McCord called Calderwood, Turner and Dharwan into his office.

"Fisher had a massive heart attack," McCord informed them, "but that's not what killed him. The fact that he had water in his lungs and bruises on his neck suggests that he was drowned."

"Hang on a minute," Calderwood said. "You're saying that Fisher, if he hadn't been murdered, would have died of a heart attack at the pond?"

"Looks like it," McCord said. "Our killer is either very unlucky or very stupid."

"Is there anything else in the report?" Calderwood asked.

"Nothing that tells us the identity of the killer," McCord said, "but something perhaps points to the reason behind the heart attack. In the inside pocket of the blazer, Crane found a letter, damp but still readable. It's from Fisher's insurance company informing him that his claim is invalid because the required smoke alarms in Roseburn House had not been properly maintained. That would be a bit of a shock right enough. We need to check with the concierge when that letter arrived, but I bet it was yesterday morning. That would explain why he didn't want to chat with his daughter."

Turner laughed. "Wouldn't it be ironic if Patrick Fisher killed him for the inheritance when he would have got it anyway?"

"It would indeed," McCord said. "That reminds me, did you check with the staff about their alibis?"

Turner nodded. "Nobody can remember much. Lunchtime is extremely busy, and they didn't pay attention to the regulars moving around. One of the waiters is sure that Danielle was at the table the whole time; oh, and there was a woman from housekeeping who picked up a bag of washing before lunch, so Danielle was in her room then. But nobody can remember anything about Patrick Fisher."

"That means, he could have sneaked out during the meal, killed his father and come back. Nobody can vouch for his whereabouts before the meal either." McCord thoughtfully stroked his chin. "What about Stuart McLellan?"

"Nobody remembers seeing him around," Dharwan said, "but he could have got in from the bottom of the garden."

"Good point," McCord said. "There is a gate leading to the Water of Leith. The crime scene investigators reported that the gate was unlocked when they arrived. There were no discernible footprints near the crime scene because the grass is very dry. At the water's edge there were damp patches, and the grass was flattened in places, but apparently that is consistent with the victim moving his arms to get his head out of the water. The killer left no clue at all. All he had to do was hold Fisher's head under the water for a couple of minutes and bingo."

"That was risky though, wasn't it?" Dharwan said. "Some guest from the hotel could have easily come that way and seen what was happening."

"True, but most of them were at lunch," McCord pointed out. "And Patrick Fisher must have been desperate. He was faced with losing his allowance and, shock horror, for the first time in his life having to earn a living, probably in a menial job."

"I understand his motive. But why McLellan?" Calderwood asked. "We thought that he might be a threat to his wife, but why to Fisher?"

"It's something Amy said," McCord reluctantly admitted. "If he married Danielle for her money, he might have wanted to speed up the process. And if he is as violent and calculating as Amy suggests, he could well be capable of cold-blooded murder. I think we should have a word with him, don't you?"

The phone rang. McCord picked up, listened, and hung up again without a word.

"Sutton has got something. Why don't you go and ask her?" McCord asked Turner with a grin.

Turner mimed a panic attack. "Please, sir, I'll do anything, but don't make me do *that*," he pleaded. "I still need to write up all these witness statements, and so does Dharwan," he added in a gesture of solidarity with his colleague.

"I don't know what's wrong with everybody," McCord said. "Sutton is brilliant. The trick is to treat her right."

He hurried across to DC Sutton's multi-level defence structure, knocked on the outer layer and went in slowly to avoid startling her.

"What have you found, DC Sutton?"

She continued typing as if he was not there.

"McLellan's unexplained income," she croaked.

McCord suspected that her vocal cords never properly warmed up because she spoke so little.

"Go on," he said encouragingly.

"Varying sums at different times and into two different accounts."

The printer began to whine. She picked up the sheet of paper that was covered in numbers. "Shred afterwards," she said. "No warrant yet."

McCord suppressed his desire to shower her with praise. He had made that mistake before and seen her cringe.

"Thank you, DC Sutton," he said instead and turned to go.

"Not finished," she said.

McCord stopped in his tracks. "Yes?"

"Lots of complaints about Fisher not paying out insurance policies."

The printer whined again.

"McLellan works for the FCA. Investigated all complaints. Fisher always cleared of wrongdoing. One complainant, a Mr Roy Sinclair, took his case to court against Simple Quote Insurance but lost."

McCord felt the delicious rush of adrenaline that always accompanied a breakthrough.

"Thank you, DC Sutton," he said again, but could not help adding, "You're a genius."

She shot him a glance as if to figure out if he was making fun of her.

"I mean it," he said to her profile. "You are my best officer."

The corners of her mouth lifted as she took a deep breath and resumed her typing.

McCord retreated quietly but swiftly. As he was leaving the barriers that Sutton had surrounded herself with, he almost bumped into Calderwood who was hovering outside.

"And?" Calderwood asked expectantly.

McCord scanned the room to check if any of the other officers were listening.

"Sutton has done it again," he said, waving the sheets of paper. "But first I need to see Gilchrist. He wants an update anyway, and while I'm there, he can authorise the application for a warrant to access McLellan's accounts. We don't want to get Sutton into trouble again."

* * *

That afternoon, McCord and Calderwood were tempted to pop into Loudons on Fountainbridge, but they had an appointment to keep across the way at the offices of the Financial Conduct Authority.

Superintendent Gilchrist, in one of his rare bouts of active involvement, had arranged for McCord and Calderwood to meet with a senior manager at the FCA, so they could determine Stuart McLellan's role within the organisation and clarify the legal and practical relationship between Police Scotland and the FCA.

"This was the topic of a seminar I attended some years ago," Gilchrist had explained, "but things change, and we need to know where we stand before we go charging in like a herd of stampeding elephants in a china shop."

The latter part of his statement had clearly been directed at McCord who ignored the snipe as well as the mixed metaphor.

"It's quite an imposing building," said Calderwood, as they walked towards the entrance.

"Do you really think so?" McCord's eyes focused on the yellowish monstrosity. "All modern fake stonework and glass. I wish I hadn't mentioned the FCA to Gilchrist at all; I bet all we're going to get is a load of waffle. If it were down to me, I'd go straight for McLellan."

Calderwood grinned. "Maybe we'll get lucky and the manager is suffering from heatstroke and can't see us."

As it turned out, it was not their lucky day.

"Ah, yes," said the receptionist once they had given their names. "Mr Rennie is expecting you. His office is down the corridor on the left. I'll let him know you're on your way."

Framed portraits of famous Scots adorned the walls of the corridor as they made their way down to the senior manager's office. McCord was amused to see 'Oor Wullie' and 'The Broons' between portraits of Robert Louis Stevenson, Sir Walter Scott and Sir Arthur Conan Doyle.

"Someone in the building seems to have an eclectic knowledge of Scottish literature," he said.

Walter Rennie turned out to be everything McCord disliked: tall, athletic and self-assured to the point of arrogance. McCord thought that the dyed-white forelock that contrasted with his still dark hair was supposed to give him gravitas, but it just made him look like a proper dandy. Rennie was definitely not responsible for the presence of 'Oor Wullie' on the corridor wall.

"Please, have a seat, detectives. Superintendent Gilchrist has asked me to give you a brief résumé of the status of the relationship between us here at the FCA and Police Scotland. I'm told you are investigating a possible case of financial fraud?"

"Yes," McCord said, already fed up with the pompous git. "We don't want to find out sometime down the line that we should have been liaising with the FCA."

Rennie leant back in his chair and crossed his legs, careful not to disturb the crisp line ironed into his trousers.

"Well, it's not quite straightforward here in Scotland. We do not have a Serious Fraud Office as they do in England and Wales, so fraud is usually your domain at Police Scotland. I thought that you would have been familiar with the legal remit of Police Scotland?"

"I'm dealing with homicides," McCord said, very much in the mood to commit one right there, right then.

Before Rennie could incense McCord further, Calderwood asked him, "So what is it the FCA does?"

Rennie puffed up his chest. "We take the lead in investigations into financial crime or regulatory misconduct usually working in tandem with other financial institutions to ensure compliance with the law."

"What does that actually mean?" McCord asked, suspecting Rennie had learned the content of their website by heart and was simply reeling it off.

Rennie regarded McCord with a condescending smile. "To put it simply, we prefer to get in early, in an advisory role. The idea is to prevent corruption and save the taxpayer the expense of potential court cases. Companies also benefit because they might avoid heavy penalties which could put them out of business. In short, prevention rather than punishment."

Against his will, McCord's interest was piqued.

"It sounds to me as if in Scotland we don't take fraud very seriously. Our Specialist Crime Division deals with other crimes as well, some more serious than fraud, and our whole police force is woefully short of manpower. Even those of us who work in Homicide could do with more officers. And then you come along, 'investigating' fraud but basically helping companies to avoid fines. The whole set-up seems very dodgy to me."

McCord felt Calderwood squirm. He was probably thinking of how Gilchrist would react if Rennie were to make a complaint. And, as always, Calderwood was not far off the mark. Rennie's complexion had turned beetroot-red.

"Now hang on, DI McCord. I will have you know that we take accusations of fraud very seriously indeed, but unfortunately, it is a legal minefield. You of all people should know how difficult it is to satisfy the procurator fiscal that there is a case to answer, and I strongly resent the suggestion that–"

"DI McCord was not implying that there is any impropriety on the FCA's part," Calderwood hastily intervened although that was exactly what McCord had been implying. "We appreciate that you are doing a great service to the legal system under challenging circumstances."

Rennie nodded, a little mollified.

"I also appreciate that you might not be allowed to comment on individual cases," Calderwood continued, "but the name of one of your employees, Stuart McLellan, has come up in a murder case we are dealing with. Can you tell us exactly what type of work he does for the FCA?"

Rennie sat up.

"Stuart? You think he might be involved in fraud – and even murder? There must have been a misunderstanding. Stuart has been a valued colleague for many years. He's a director of enforcement here at the FCA, which means he ensures that financial institutions operate according to the law."

McCord frowned.

"What about his investigation into complaints that Simple Quote Insurance was not honouring claims made against house insurance policies? Our own investigation has discovered that Stuart McLellan was the FCA employee who gave Simple Quote a clean bill of health."

Rennie shrugged.

"I have every confidence in Stuart. If he found that no laws had been broken, that will be right. But give me a moment. I'll quickly look up our records of that case."

"And what about a possible conflict of interest?" McCord asked. "After all, at the time of his investigation he was engaged to the daughter of the owner of Simple Quote. Surely, he should not have been tasked with that particular case!"

"We have a very strict policy on conflicts of interest, and all submissions are carefully scrutinised and monitored," Rennie said while bringing up the file. "Ah, here we are. Yes, I remember now. If you had done your own investigations thoroughly, you would have learned that the daughter had absolutely nothing to do with her father's insurance company. Indeed, it says here she was a beautician."

"She was," McCord said, "but she was still the daughter of the owner of the company your organisation was tasked to investigate. If that's not a conflict of interest, I don't know what is!"

At that, Rennie stood up, leaning on the desk.

"DI McCord! You're obviously unaware of the fact that FCA policy does not require disclosure of a sibling or child whose job does not come under the remit of the FCA or whose business is not authorised by the FCA. You must also remember that there was a court case, and the judge found no evidence of criminality by Simple Quote or any impropriety in the conduct of the FCA."

Calderwood lifted his hands in an appeasing gesture.

"As I've said, Mr Rennie, there is no suggestion of wrongdoing on the part of the FCA. DI McCord and I are merely trying to understand how the system works."

Rennie gave McCord a dirty look and sat down again.

"I stand by all I have said about Stuart McLellan. Indeed, he is very thorough in all he does and has followed the letter of the law in every single case he has been given. You need have no worries about him. As a matter of fact, Stuart is about to be honoured for his work in combatting cybercrime. He is an absolute genius–"

"Cybercrime?" McCord butted in. "We were under the impression that he worked on financial fraud."

Rennie shook his head.

"He did, but that was years ago. The real growth area is cybercrime, online dealings which cause thousands and sometimes millions of pounds to be siphoned off at the click of a button into some offshore bank account. Tracking where the money has gone and into whose account is devilishly difficult, and that's where Stuart and his colleagues' expertise comes in."

McCord realised that this conversation was getting them nowhere. He was quietly seething at the corruption he suspected to be festering in this legal grey zone, but he was confident that DC Sutton would get to the bottom of it. He rose from his seat.

"We'd still like a word with your esteemed director of enforcement. Where can we find him?"

Rennie sighed.

"I'll show you. Please follow me."

As they climbed the stairs to the floor above, Calderwood made pleasant small talk with Rennie, while McCord was planning his attack on McLellan.

Chapter 18

Stuart McLellan's grey face lost even the last remnants of colour when his boss ushered him into a small conference room with two detectives and cheerfully left him to answer their questions. While Calderwood stood up and greeted McLellan politely, McCord remained seated, his elbows on the table, his chin resting on his folded hands.

McLellan adjusted his perfectly positioned tie and the creases in the trousers of his slate grey suit before he took the seat opposite. McCord was always dressed neatly, but in this institution wearing a suit was taken to a new level. Were the absurdly straight ties and creases there to compensate for their otherwise crooked dealings? Before he had finished his train of thought,

Calderwood cleared his throat indicating that he was ready with his notebook.

"Now, Mr McLellan, do you know why we might want to speak to you?" McCord began.

McLellan shook his head. "I have absolutely no idea," he said.

Even his voice lacked any vibrance. McCord found it difficult to imagine this shadow of a man committing the acts against women Dolly had confirmed, let alone the ones Amy suspected him of. McCord detested nothing more than violence against women, but he reminded himself that this was not the main reason why they were here.

"No idea?" McCord echoed. "That surprises me. After all, there are so many reasons why we have the pleasure of meeting you here today. Let's begin with the most straightforward one. Could you please confirm, Mr McLellan, that between 2001 and 2013 you took bribes from Morton Fisher, to help him avoid a conviction for the fraud he committed as the owner of Simple Quote Insurance? We have the whole paper trail here" – he patted the folder in front of him affectionately – "but it would be nice to hear it from you personally."

McLellan turned a greenish shade of grey and defiantly folded his arms.

"You don't need to say anything at all," McCord continued. "You can nod if I get this right. Morton Fisher created a subsidiary of his legitimate insurance firm which channelled the premiums into a Swiss bank account. Thanks to some carefully worded clauses in the contracts, clients making a claim found that it was rejected. Several of them complained, but the FCA always concluded that the law had not been broken. You will be aware that some cynical members of the press call your employer the Fundamentally Complicit Authority, so it seems that you are not alone."

McLellan gave a theatrical sigh. "Surely, you are not basing your investigation on some article in *Private Eye*? Their editor seems to have an unhealthy obsession with big business and unfortunately with us here at the FCA. Mind you, he is never out of court with all the litigation cases against him."

"Don't worry," McCord said, "we are not here to drain the whole swamp; it's your little patch that interests us. I have to say that I am astounded that no conflict of interest was identified which might have prevented you from being the lead person in that investigation. That arrangement with your father-in-law was very convenient for both of you, wasn't it? He became very rich, and you, the investigating officer, pocketed a substantial amount over the years."

McLellan shook his head. "Not true."

McCord ignored the remark.

"This nice little scam only stopped when a certain Roy Sinclair took Fisher to court, and although he lost even in the appeal, more and more people started asking questions. Eventually, all the negative publicity made Fisher nervous, so he sold Simple Quote and made off with the money. I hear you are a computer expert, so you would have been the perfect person to help Fisher hide his ill-gotten gains away from the prying eyes of the police and the taxman. How am I doing so far?"

Not a muscle moved in McLellan's face as he said, "You have an enviable imagination. Maybe you should be writing novels, like my brother-in-law, rather than investigating non-existent crime. If you were to study our statistics, you would learn that the FCA does not always fine the businesses it has investigated. And the reason for that is not that we are complicit in any crimes, as some organs of the press repeatedly claim; it's because we have to find evidence and follow the law – principles you should be familiar with, DI McCord."

"Then how do you explain the considerable sums of money paid to you even now from accounts that are very difficult to trace?"

McLellan smiled smugly. "The last time I looked, it was no crime for a generous man to transfer money to his son-in-law. Surely, it is up to him which accounts he uses for that."

"We'll leave that to our Specialist Crime Division to decide, shall we?" McCord said. "And I'll make sure that the case is not handed back to the FCA to investigate itself." He knew he was losing ground here. McLellan was a far harder nut to crack than he had thought.

"However, there is another thing we are interested in," he pressed on. "And this is your relationship with your wife."

For the first time, McLellan showed some emotion. "Whatever she has told you, she is lying. Unfortunately, Danielle is mentally unstable."

McCord did not even blink. "Your wife hasn't told us anything. A concerned member of the public has drawn our attention to the scars and bruises on her legs."

McLellan's eyes narrowed. "Which member of the public?" he asked.

"I'm not at liberty to say," McCord replied.

"Well, tell your concerned busybody to keep their big nose out of other people's private lives, especially when they don't know what they're talking about."

McCord and Calderwood could not help grinning at the mention of Amy's nose.

McLellan bristled. "What are you laughing at?"

"Nothing," McCord said. "Domestic violence is no laughing matter as far as I'm concerned. And I find it interesting that Hunter prefers the company of his mentally unstable mother to yours."

For the first time, McLellan raised his voice. "It's purely because she has poisoned his mind against me," he shouted. "That's why I sent him to Cargilfield School as a weekly boarder, to protect him from all that!"

McCord pretended to contemplate this possibility.

"Be that as it may, but if we ever hear of your wife, or any other woman, for example a prostitute, suffering any injuries after an encounter with you, or if there are complaints about stalking, we will be coming after you very promptly. Have I made myself clear?"

McLellan sneered with contempt. "This is ridiculous. Fraud, assault, stalking, soliciting – you'll be accusing me of murder next."

McCord smiled grimly.

"It's interesting that you should mention murder," he said. "That is precisely the next thing I was going to ask you about. Where were you yesterday morning between eleven thirty and one o'clock?"

McCord noted with satisfaction the red blotches forming on McLellan's face.

"Murder?" he spluttered. "What are you on about?"

"Yesterday, lunchtime. That's the time your father-in-law was murdered. His death makes your wife a wealthy heiress, which is why you married her in the first place, is it not?"

McLellan jumped up. "That is an outrageous suggestion! You have no evidence of that!"

Calderwood moved swiftly out of his chair to stop him, but it was not necessary.

"Sit down, Mr McLellan," McCord ordered in his dangerous quiet voice that never failed to have the desired effect.

McLellan slowly did as he was told.

"That's better. I'm asking you again, Mr McLellan, where were you yesterday between eleven thirty and one o'clock?"

"I feel I should not answer any more of your ridiculous questions without having one of our lawyers with me, but for the record, and since I have nothing to hide, I was having lunch at Loudons across the way. You can check that with their staff – I am well known there."

"You can rest assured we will go and do that right now," McCord said, getting up. "Don't leave the city without letting us know. Goodbye, Mr McLellan. Have a nice day."

Chapter 19

The following morning, McCord carefully stacked the witness statements in front of him with a big grin on his face.

"Nobody at Loudons remembers McLellan having lunch there two days ago, which means he was lying, which means he is in the frame for Fisher's murder."

"Hang on a moment," Calderwood objected. "We can't be certain of that. If you read the statements carefully, you'll see that they were all unsure whether he was there or not. He is, after all, a regular customer and not somebody you'd look at twice. Nobody was prepared to say with any degree of certainty that he was *not* there."

McCord was deflated but his disappointment was brief. "You are splitting hairs, Calderwood. The fact remains that he has no alibi."

"It is also a fact that we have no forensic evidence to link McLellan to the crime scene, no witnesses and no confession. The timing is also tight although his colleagues were unsure about when exactly he left or returned at lunchtime."

"He is like The Invisible Man," McCord said. "I believe he could murder somebody on Princes Street in broad daylight, and still nobody would notice him."

A decisive knock on the door interrupted their conversation.

"Come in," McCord shouted, expecting Turner or Dharwan to bring some good news.

But it wasn't either of them coming in. It was trouble.

"Hello, Duncan," Amy greeted Calderwood warmly. "Hello, McCord," she added, about ten degrees cooler. "I was wondering how you were getting on with catching Morton Fisher's killer. The good citizens of Edinburgh are fearful that a serial killer is on the loose and that they're not safe in their grossly overpriced homes."

"A fear that has been magnified by your colleagues from the gutter press," McCord pointed out. "I'm surprised it took you so long to pop in and share your wisdom with us. Normally, you start to interfere before the body is even cold."

"That's because, without my interference, you never seem to get anywhere. While you've been bumbling about in the dark, I have done some research and found you a suspect with a cracker of a motive."

"Really."

Since Amy's assumption that he was using prostitutes, McCord's expectations of her theories were even lower than before.

"And that would be a better motive than a massive inheritance or covering up a crime?" he said. "Because we have two suspects that applies to and neither of them has an alibi."

"Let's hear what Amy has to say, shall we?" Calderwood butted in.

Amy, however, did not need any intervention to hold her own against McCord. "My suspect has a better motive than anybody out there. His name is Roy Sinclair–"

"Sorry to disappoint you," McCord interrupted, "but we bumbling PC Plods know about him already. He was one of the victims of Fisher's insurance scam. He took Simple Quote to court but lost. That was years ago. Sorry, Amy, our suspects trump yours."

Amy regarded McCord with a mixture of pity and exasperation.

"No, they most certainly do not. Are you going to listen to me, or do you not even wish to hear what I have to say?"

McCord sighed. "On you go then."

Amy settled into the chair opposite McCord.

"Roy Sinclair wasn't the victim at all; it was his brother. He was very close to him and his family. Their house burnt down, and Fisher's insurance company refused to pay. It ruined them. The brother's wife had a debilitating illness and died in unsuitable rented accommodation a few months after the fire, and the brother killed himself shortly afterwards. Sinclair fought the court battle on their behalf even after their deaths and spent all his savings on lawyers' fees. Isn't it poetic justice to burn down Fisher's house and then drown him?"

"And you got all this from...?"

"From the archives of my colleagues in the gutter press which you despise so much," Amy said, slapping a file on the desk. "But you still haven't heard the best part."

"And what is that?" McCord asked, still sceptical.

"The day of the fire at Roseburn House was the anniversary of the fire that destroyed Sinclair's family."

"Wow," Calderwood said, "that is too much of a coincidence. Well done, Amy. Hasn't she done brilliantly?" he added, looking pointedly at McCord.

"It might be worth checking out," McCord admitted grudgingly.

There was a knock on the door.

"Come in!"

If McCord had hoped for moral support from Turner or Dharwan, he was disappointed.

It was DS Struthers. As he took in the scene, his face contorted into a smutty grin and his greedy eyes settled on Amy. McCord had no doubt that the prime purpose of Struthers's visit was to garner some intelligence on how the relationship between Amy and McCord was progressing to pass it on to colleagues who were continuously speculating about this hot topic.

"Yes, DS Struthers, what do you want?" McCord barked. "We are kind of busy right now."

"I'm sure you are, sir," Struthers said with that note of insolence in his voice that he had never quite managed to lose, even under McCord's leadership. "That's why I was wondering perhaps if you had a job that I could get stuck into."

McCord could not believe what the DS was saying.

"We are dealing with an arson attack that killed a woman, and a homicide. I should think that there is plenty to do for everybody. But if you are struggling, DS Struthers, find me the court files of an insurance claim – Sinclair versus Simple Quote Insurance – and report back to me asap."

Surely, even someone with intellectual powers as limited as Struthers's could not mess this up.

"If that's what you want, sir," Struthers said with a sour face. "But I would have thought that this was a task more suited to an officer of lower rank."

"If you are thinking of PC Dharwan and PC Turner, they are busy." Doing real police work, he added silently. "I expect to have your report by lunchtime today."

Struthers withdrew in a huff, but at least he withdrew.

When the door had firmly closed behind him, Calderwood picked up the folder that Amy had brought and looked at McCord.

"Why don't you two go for a coffee while I update the Fisher file with Amy's findings and try to verify the story?"

McCord glared at Calderwood. "I've got two unsolved murders on my patch. I don't have time for that."

"Surely, you could do with a coffee yourself, Duncan," Amy said. "I'd love a quick chat."

"Calderwood hasn't got time either," McCord snapped. "We'll check out this guy Sinclair, but my money is still on one of the other two."

"Please yourself," Amy said and, on her way out, slammed the door shut.

McCord stared at it trembling in its frame. He suppressed the sudden desire to kick it down but instead, slumped back in his chair.

Calderwood looked at him full of reproach.

"If you want a coffee break, go ahead, and while you're at it, get me one as well," McCord said by way of an apology.

Calderwood shook his head. "It's not about that."

"No, you're right. It's about you, acting like a dating agency. I saw what you were doing there. Stop it, DS Calderwood."

"As you wish, sir," Calderwood said with an expressionless face. As he left, he gently closed the door behind him.

McCord kicked the leg of the desk and swore as pain seared through his big toe. Why did people have to be so bloody difficult?

* * *

Unsurprisingly, it was late afternoon by the time Struthers reported back on the Sinclair versus Simple Quote Insurance case.

"There were two court cases," he whined when McCord asked him about the delay, "the original one and then the appeal. It was all very tedious, with lawyers going into every detail of the contract."

"I'm so sorry you were not sufficiently entertained by your task, DS Struthers," McCord said, but his sarcasm bounced off Struthers's inflated ego. "Have you learned anything at all from the files that might help us build a case against Sinclair?"

"Well," Struthers began in his irritatingly slow manner, "what really caught my attention was that Sinclair made a death threat against Morton Fisher after he had lost the appeal."

McCord jumped up.

"Really? What did he say?"

"He said" – Struthers flicked through his notes – "quote, 'You will pay for this, Fisher. My brother died because of your greed and corruption, and you will burn for it!'"

Struthers lowered the sheet of paper. "The judge reprimanded Sinclair at the time and warned him not to take matters into his own hands, but she let him off with a verbal warning, 'considering the circumstances of the case'."

"The judge must have been frustrated that there was not enough evidence to convict Fisher and she probably had a lot of sympathy for Sinclair," McCord said. "But now it looks as if her kindness had fatal consequences. Calderwood!" he shouted into the corridor.

Like a flash, Calderwood was by his side.

"Come on! You and I are off to see Sinclair. Well done, DS Struthers," McCord said. "That's a good piece of work. Add it to the case file."

As McCord and Calderwood headed for the exit, neither of them noticed Struthers jealously staring at them.

* * *

Roy Sinclair lived in a tiny but tidy flat on Gorgie Road. When McCord and Calderwood appeared at his door and showed their IDs, he seemed surprised when they asked him politely if they could come in. He opened the door wide and led them wordlessly into a stuffy living room.

"Tea?" he asked. "I don't have coffee."

"We're fine, thanks," Calderwood said with his winning smile. "We would like to ask you a few questions about your brother if you don't mind."

McCord should have been used to Calderwood's ways by now, but he still marvelled at his partner's impeccable manners and genuine good nature. He himself, unfettered by convention, was having a look round.

In one corner of the room, Sinclair had erected a veritable altar. On a beautifully embroidered tablecloth, photographs with black crêpe wound round the frames stood in front of a fresh bunch of carnations and a simple wooden cross. One was a wedding photograph of a smiling young couple, another showed the same man about ten years older next to a woman sitting in a wheelchair. The whole arrangement seemed a little haphazard and one corner of the tablecloth had got caught in the drawer underneath.

Sinclair said nothing. His bushy, horizontal eyebrows almost met above the bridge of his nose and shaded a pair of deep blue eyes that were watching McCord's every move. His dark, leathery skin was witness to a life spent largely outdoors, and the square chin indicated somebody who was not easily pushed off a chosen course. Sinclair seemed cautious, rather than frightened, as he waited for the detectives to begin their questioning.

"We understand that your brother and his wife took out an insurance policy with Simple Quote," Calderwood said, "and that the company refused to pay out when they had a house fire?"

"Correct," Sinclair said. "At first, the insurance company claimed my brother and his wife had not used due diligence because one of the smoke alarm batteries was dead and my brother had not tried to contain the small fire."

He laughed bitterly. "It was a joke: my brother was in the kitchen when the toaster exploded, so the smoke alarms that did go off in the hall and in the living room made no difference at all. He had no equipment to put out even a small fire and was preoccupied anyway with getting his sick wife out of the house as quickly as he could. When the lawyer pointed this out to Simple Quote, they changed tack and revealed that my brother had signed a contract with a subsidiary of the company which operated independently. The FCA said that no laws were broken and that my brother should have read the small print in the contract more carefully. To cut a very long story short: after paying into the insurance for ten years, they didn't get any money when they needed it."

"And after your brother passed away, you continued to fight the case?" Calderwood asked gently.

"My brother didn't *pass away*," Sinclair hissed, "he hanged himself because those bastards took his money all those years and then left him high and dry. He adored Jeanie, my sister-in-law, and struggled on in a flat that was hopeless for somebody in a wheelchair. He became very depressed, and when she died, he simply gave up on life."

"Are you aware of a man called Morton Fisher?" Calderwood asked.

"Of course. I know all about Morton Fisher," Sinclair said. "He died the day before yesterday."

"He was the owner of Simple Quote Insurance; did you know that?"

"I did," Sinclair said, but his face gave nothing away. "During the court case, the lawyer told me he was sure that Fisher was behind the scheme but that there was no legal way of getting to him."

"Did you know that Fisher's house was burnt down Saturday before last, on the very anniversary of the fire at your brother's house?" Calderwood asked.

Sinclair nodded slowly. "I read about it in the papers."

By now, McCord had lost patience with Calderwood's softly-softly approach.

"Let's not pussyfoot around, Mr Sinclair. We know that you threatened Fisher in court. 'You will burn', I think, were the words you used."

Sinclair said nothing, but a little smile twitched around his mouth, a reaction McCord had not expected. Surely, Sinclair could not be as arrogant as this. Or was he perhaps proud of what he had done?

"You can surely see where we are going with this, Mr Sinclair," McCord said. "Where were you at the times of the fire and the murder?"

Sinclair turned to Calderwood for help.

"I don't have to answer any questions, do I?"

Calderwood shook his head. "No, you don't, Mr Sinclair."

McCord glared at Calderwood, so he quickly continued. "But it would be much better for you if you fully cooperated with us. I'm sure any judge would take into account all the events leading up to the arson and the murder. You should call a lawyer."

"I've already handed all my money over to the legal profession, and a fat lot of good it did me," Sinclair said. "Are you going to arrest me?"

Calderwood looked at his boss.

"Yes, Mr Sinclair," McCord said. "I am going to charge you, but before I do so I must caution you that you do not need to say anything in answer to the charge but anything you do say will be noted and may be used in evidence. Do you understand?"

Sinclair had listened attentively. "I understand. Can I pack a bag before we go?"

"I'm not finished," McCord said irritably. "The charge against you is that you committed arson leading to the death of Victoria Norval, resident at Roseburn House, and that you murdered Morton Fisher at The Braemar Hotel on Monday, 26 June this year."

"I understand," Sinclair repeated. "Now, can I pack my bag?"

"Yes, you can," McCord said. "But DS Calderwood will have to go with you."

"There is no need for him to do that. I'm not going to climb through the bathroom window or top myself," Sinclair said, "but please yourselves."

While they were away, McCord had another look around. One wall was taken up by bookshelves with a range of religious literature; from the titles, McCord concluded that Sinclair was a Catholic. Another case that proved that religion did not stop people from murdering each other. He picked up the well-thumbed *Guide to British Birds* sitting next to some illustrated books about the 282 Munros of Scotland. He had more doubts about a birdwatcher or a Munro-bagger being a killer, than he had about a devout churchgoer, but he knew he was biased. McCord was convinced that anybody could kill given the right circumstances, and it was clear that Sinclair and his brother had been let down by everybody who should have given them justice.

A few minutes later, Sinclair, with Calderwood right behind him, returned with a small holdall.

"Can I take some books with me?" Sinclair asked.

"I don't see why not," McCord said.

From the coffee table, Sinclair picked up his Bible, a couple of religious books and the biography of Ernest Shackleton by Ranulph Fiennes.

"I'm ready now," he said, and walked towards the hallway followed by Calderwood and McCord. Outside on the landing, it took him a while to insert the key into the lock. "Arthritis," he explained.

As they were about to descend the stairs, he hesitated.

"I wonder if I could take a minute to speak to my neighbour?" he asked.

Calderwood waited for a nod of confirmation from McCord. "Fine."

Sinclair rang the bell, and they waited until they heard a shuffling sound inside and a chain being slid back. An old woman opened the door.

"How many times have I told you, Marge, not to open the door without asking who is there," Sinclair scolded her. "You never know – somebody might be out to rob you."

"Ach, stop your whingeing," the woman called Marge replied robustly. "What is the matter? Who are these two gentlemen?"

"They're from the police, Marge. I've been arrested."

Marge, arms akimbo, looked from McCord to Calderwood. "You are arresting Roy? Surely not because that scumbag Fisher finally got what was coming to him?"

"It's okay, Marge," Sinclair said hastily. "There is a bunch of flowers in the lounge and food in the fridge. I might be gone a while, and it would be a shame to waste them. I just wanted to let you know so that you don't worry."

"Not worry?" Marge shrieked. "And what about–"

"Please take care of the place for me, will you?" Sinclair asked and started down the stairs. "Bye, Marge, take care."

The old woman's muttering followed them all way down to the main door. Sinclair seemed relieved when it closed noisily into the lock behind them.

The journey back through the city centre from Gorgie Road to St Leonard's was as tortuous as always, and McCord asked himself for the umpteenth time why he had chosen to live in this city that was designed to drive perfectly nice people insane.

The bus lanes were free, as usual, and he was tempted to put the flashing blue light on the car roof and overtake all other traffic. With no emergency to respond to, however, such an action might lead to him having to answer awkward questions from his superiors, namely Gilchrist. And how the Super would love that!

There were simply too many people in the city, and too many cars. McCord wondered why it had never occurred to him before. It was so obvious: that was the reason why there were so many murders in Edinburgh. Nobody ever got killed in peaceful, uncongested Oban. But then, very few people wanted to live there although it was great for birdwatching...

"Sir?" Calderwood dragged McCord out of his muddled musings. "Amy has sent a text asking how we got on with... you know. What shall I say?"

McCord grunted and looked in the back mirror at their prisoner. Sinclair was sitting quietly, staring out of the window at the city baking in the midday heat.

"Tell her what happened, and I suppose I'll have to suffer her gloating next time she turns up at the station, which no doubt won't be long."

The return to St Leonard's should have been a triumphal procession, like Roman generals dragging their captives behind them on their victory parade. McCord, however, was anything but jubilant, and he knew why: it would have been so much more fun to have nabbed Stuart McLellan.

Chapter 20

The news of the arrest had spread through the city like wildfire. In the office of *Forth Write* magazine, Amy was sitting hunched over her laptop, chewing on her thumb. John wanted the first draft of the supplement tonight, and the final version tomorrow, ready for the printer. The story should have written itself. After all, she had been there right from the start through all its twists and turns, and, as usual, it had been her who had unearthed the information that led to Roy Sinclair's arrest.

And yet, the words that normally flowed with such ease refused to come. What the readers loved, and had missed during her travels in Europe, was her special relationship with Edinburgh CID and her unique insight into the workings of the police. With growing unease, she came to realise that her articles had not been about her; they had been about her and McCord hunting down killers.

The unspoken deal with Gilchrist was that she could enjoy unprecedented access to the station in return for a favourable report on its workings. It had always been easy to praise McCord and his team, who were dedicated to the point of obsession and investigated without fear or favour to protect the citizens of Edinburgh. The customary praise bestowed on Gilchrist had been insincere but necessary to secure this arrangement which worked to everybody's satisfaction even if McCord pretended it did not.

McCord... she thought. It was all McCord's fault. He had not even bothered to tell her about Sinclair's arrest. If she hadn't contacted Duncan, she would have been reduced to relying on the rumours swirling about. Amy now found herself running after the pack, rather than leading it. That was it: she was simply choking on the words which might show McCord in a positive light. The hero of the Diamond Murders case had turned out to be a deeply flawed man who showed no interest at all in her, Amy Thornton, nor in her ideas. Flirting with gardeners, associating with – she did not even want to finish that thought – and entirely without any acknowledgment of her vital contributions, he did not appreciate her. One had to preserve one's dignity. One had to make a stand. This would be her last piece on Edinburgh CID. Full stop. The end. At least her mother would be happy.

"What is the matter with you, darling? You're bleeding!"

Martin, clad in an outfit inspired by 1970s hippiedom, had fluttered across to her desk, a restorative latte in his long, clawlike fingers.

Amy looked at the teeth marks on her thumb that had blood seeping out of them and burst into tears. Martin carefully put down the steaming coffee, pulled her up into his arms and rocked her back and forth like a child. When her sobbing subsided, he sat her down again, pulled up a chair for himself and took hold of her hands. His precisely plucked, impossibly black eyebrows were raised underneath a forehead furrowed with anxiety.

"What on earth has happened to upset you so much?"

And then it all poured out of her – everything, even the devastating conversation with Dolly.

Amy had expected one of Martin's overwrought twitterings, but to her surprise, he was completely calm.

"DI McCord, as we all know, does lack a certain *je-ne-sais-quoi*, but we also know that he put his life on the line for you."

"Did he, though?" Amy hiccupped. "He would do anything to catch a killer, maybe me being there was pure coincidence."

"I'm sure it wasn't," Martin said. "And even if he sought solace in the arms of a lady of the night, who are we to judge? I understand he has been on his own for a long time. Relationships are difficult in a job like his, and especially for a man like him. He needs friends who support him, not people who sit on a high horse and convict him before he has even had a chance to say his piece."

Amy pulled her hands away to blow her nose. "He has had a chance, two chances in fact, but he did not take them."

"DI McCord is not somebody who finds it easy to talk about his feelings. Maybe he doesn't even fully understand them himself."

"Whatever, but he is a bloody pain in the neck," Amy said, chucking the tissue in the bin.

Martin smiled. "I suspect he says exactly the same about you. Come on, you are a pro. Get this article done. The next murder will come along like sunshine after the rain, and you two can have a new start."

Amy gave Martin a kiss on his rouged cheek.

"Maybe. You're right. I can do this. And tomorrow I'll go and see Danielle McLellan. That husband of hers is not going to get away with abusing a woman and destroying the childhood of that poor little boy."

Chapter 21

When McCord reached St Leonard's in the morning, a crowd of reporters had already gathered at the entrance in the hope of further news. The morning papers had gone mad. Screaming headlines about the Avenging Arsonist and the Murrayfield Murderer promised all the gory details of a tale that had everything the rainbow press loved: fire, revenge and death. The sympathies were split; the right-wing papers, very much in favour of law and order, thundered about the outrage of vigilantism, while the lefties pointed to the failure of the system to protect the little guy against ruthless fat cats.

Roy Sinclair was the one person in all of Edinburgh who had nothing to say about the whole affair. Despite the efforts of his well-meaning duty solicitor, he refused to comment. Out of the three main suspects, he was the only one who did not refute the charges but in common with the others, there was no forensic evidence that might influence a jury to convict.

Superintendent Gilchrist had vented his frustration on McCord, urging him to do something. What exactly he expected McCord to do, he was unable to say; apparently, it was McCord's job to figure that out.

As McCord returned to his office, fuming as always after an encounter with Gilchrist, he found a visitor there. Everything about that man reminded him of a greyhound: the pointed, elongated face and chin, as well as the absurdly long and thin limbs. On seeing McCord, he put down a plastic cup filled with the station's ghastly tea that Calderwood had supplied him with. The greyhound shifted nervously on his chair as if waiting for a starter pistol to go off.

"Mr Basset here is a friend of Mr Sinclair's and he has come in to make a statement," Calderwood informed McCord, who was having difficulty covering up his laugh with a cough.

The effort brought tears to his eyes, and it took him a moment to recover his composure, which was completely destroyed as soon as Basset lifted his head, looked up to the ceiling and opened his mouth. The sentence started with a brief, high-pitched whine that eventually descended into a low soprano and ended on a flat C.

McCord buried his face in his handkerchief, emitting a choking noise. He had not had such a fit of hysterics since he was a teenager. It had to be the stress of dealing with a double murder as well as Gilchrist's overbearing incompetence.

"Are you alright, Inspector?" Basset asked, visibly concerned.

Calderwood noisily cleared his throat.

"Mr Basset told me earlier that he is prepared to swear on the Bible that he was with Mr Sinclair during the time Mr Fisher was murdered."

"What?" McCord gasped, his hysterics over as suddenly as they had appeared. "You're saying that Roy Sinclair has an alibi for the time of Morton Fisher's murder?"

"That's exactly what I've been saying," Basset whined, a note of irritation in his voice. "We climbed two Munros including Ben Lawers that day and had a couple of drinks in the hotel afterwards. I could not believe it when I read in the paper this morning that he had been arrested, so I came straight over."

McCord suppressed an oath. But there was still some hope.

"What about the fire at Roseburn House?"

"I don't know where he was then," Basset said, "but I am convinced it was not him. Roy is a man of God. He has principles."

In McCord's experience those were also the characteristics of terrorists and many famous serial killers, but he thought it wise not to comment.

"Mr Basset, DS Calderwood will take your statement now. Thank you for coming in."

He left the office and paced up and down the corridor, trying to get rid of his pent-up frustration. They were back to square one.

* * *

Once Basset had left, McCord called a staff meeting.

"Roy Sinclair has an alibi for the time of Morton Fisher's murder" – a groan went around the room – "but he is still very much in the frame for the arson attack. If it was him, then Victoria Norval's death was likely unintentional. At best we can get him for arson and involuntary manslaughter, if we find any evidence or witnesses, that is. PC Dharwan, take the mugshots of Sinclair and check with the neighbours again around Roseburn House on the off chance somebody saw him that day."

"Yes, sir," Dharwan said.

"This scenario would mean that Fisher's murder was unconnected to the fire. The most likely suspects now are his children, who were expecting a sizeable inheritance because they probably did not know that the house insurance had been invalidated. The daughter, Danielle McLellan, was with Hunter at the time of the murder, but Patrick Fisher cannot account for the time before lunch, and he also left the table during the meal. We know that he was angry with his father for planning to end his allowance and, with it, his very comfortable lifestyle. We need to interview him again and try to crack him."

McCord turned to the incident board. "However, there is also Stuart McLellan, Fisher's son-in-law, whom we suspect of controlling and abusing his wife, Danielle. McLellan had two reasons for wanting Fisher dead: firstly, to cover up Fisher's insurance fraud that he was most certainly complicit in, and secondly to get to Danielle's inheritance more quickly. His alibi is shaky, and if he went from his office to The Braemar to kill Fisher, there might be CCTV footage of him going there. Unsurprisingly, he denies all of this. PC Turner, you get onto that."

Turner nodded.

"But then," McCord continued, "let's not forget James Palmer-Wycliffe, who is currently enjoying our hospitality for his involvement in drug dealing and money laundering. He was already in a police cell when Fisher was murdered, but he also had a strong motive for killing Victoria Norval. He claims that he drove straight from his parents' estate near Balerno to Roseburn House but that the fire was already raging when he arrived. We do need to check any traffic cameras on his route back along the Lanark Road. Maybe we can prove that he was in the area earlier than he says he was."

He pointed to the pictures on the incident board.

"Three suspects, each one of them capable of murder."

McCord saw a hand going up, and his heart sank. "Yes, DS Struthers?"

Struthers stood up so that everybody could see and hear him.

"There is another possible scenario, sir," he said, "that would mean that both murders are linked."

"Which is?"

"Someone else who was defrauded by Fisher's insurance scam took revenge by burning down the house and then murdered him when the first attempt failed."

"That is a possibility," McCord conceded, sensing a great opportunity to keep Struthers out of the way for the next few days. "It means going through all the clients of Simple Quote Insurance and its subsidiary and finding anybody who would have a similar grievance. The claim would have to be for a considerable sum, however, for someone to go to such extreme lengths, so concentrate on those claims involving many thousands, possibly hundreds of thousands of pounds." McCord grinned. "Thank you for volunteering, DS Struthers, I'll leave that in your and DC Sutton's capable hands. If you liaise with her, you'll find she can save you a lot of time."

A wave of suppressed glee went through the room as everybody imagined Struthers having to enter Sutton's den. McCord had been aware of her following the briefing from the back by the wall, as far away as possible from everybody else. Her anxious expression had given way to outright panic at the mention of Struthers.

A wave of affection for his troubled hacker washed over McCord and he decided to forego the fun he was going to have watching Struthers circling the den in fear. "DC Sutton, if you give the information you find to me, I'll pass it on to DS Struthers."

He was moved by the look of gratitude she gave him, which even made up for the relief on Struthers's face.

"Right, I want witness statements and CCTV checked and double-checked. The killer or killers must have made a mistake, and we need to find it."

Chapter 22

When Amy entered the lobby of The Braemar, she spotted Patrick Fisher in an armchair at the back, nursing a double whisky. She was here to see Danielle, but maybe she could persuade him to give her something on McLellan, and, she realised to her own surprise, she regretted the way they had parted the previous week.

He was engrossed in something on his phone, and at first, she thought he was scrolling down a file, but then she saw that he was stroking across the screen, backwards and forwards as if he could not make up his mind about something.

She walked up to him quietly, and when she spoke, he almost jumped out of his seat.

"Sorry if I gave you a fright," Amy said, "I wasn't aware that I looked so awful this morning."

He failed to come up with a complimentary riposte; in fact, he did not say anything at all.

She lowered herself into the armchair opposite him and crossed her legs whose shape was enhanced rather than obscured by her silky dress. She noticed that he noticed, and smiled. "I'm sorry that we parted on bad terms last time. I just wanted to help your sister."

Patrick's eyes met hers. "I believe you. But first Victoria, then Dad..."

"It must have been difficult," Amy said. "How are you holding up?"

Patrick Fisher took another swig of his malt.

"It's a nightmare. The phone doesn't stop ringing with bloody hacks, present company excepted, of course" – he bowed slightly in her direction – "all wanting an interview. Thank God, they've stopped camping outside the hotel now."

"You must be pleased that the police have arrested that guy Sinclair," Amy said.

"Of course."

Amy expected Patrick Fisher to say more but he did not. "Quite a tragic case," she continued. "It seems that your father's fraudulent activities ruined Sinclair's brother and drove him to suicide. Sinclair devoted years of his life and all his savings to get justice through the official channels but failed. He then decided to take the law into his own hands and killed your father."

Patrick Fisher put down his whisky glass with a clonk.

"That is terrible," he said. "I had no idea."

"How is your sister?" Amy asked, coming back to her original reason for this conversation.

"It's been hard," Patrick Fisher said, "especially on Hunter. He's not been the same since."

Amy nodded. "Is he getting any counselling?"

Patrick Fisher laughed bitterly. "I've been in touch with Children's Services. They had a chat with him and concluded he was fine for now. Problems were more likely to occur in puberty, they said, and to come back when things got worse."

Amy shook her head in disbelief.

"That is pathetic, but I suppose they're overwhelmed with cases. Can you not go private?"

Patrick Fisher shifted uncomfortably in his seat. "All of Dad's accounts are frozen until the estate is settled, so I have no money coming in. The solicitor says it could be a year before we see any of it. A year! Why would it take so bloody long? The hotel manager has been to see me and asked very politely when the bills for our rooms will be settled. He was not happy with my answer."

"I'm sure you'll find a job soon," Amy said. "Maybe even in journalism?"

"Is there a vacancy at your magazine?"

"I'm afraid not," Amy said, "but you could try the daily papers. And maybe being famous now will help to get your novel accepted by a big publisher."

"Famous? Notorious, more like," Patrick Fisher said, running his hand through his hair and making it stand up in all directions. "I've come to accept that my family is right about the first novel. It is rubbish, but I know I can write a better one. My main problem at the moment is… I can't get my head around anything at all."

A waiter approached discreetly and asked Amy if she would like a drink.

She sensed that Patrick Fisher wanted to be on his own and that she was not going to find an ally in her fight for Danielle here.

"No, thank you," Amy said, "I have to be on my way."

She turned to Patrick Fisher. "As you said, it's been a hard time for you all. I'm sure things will get better soon. Bye for now."

"Goodbye," Patrick Fisher said. "I'm sorry."

What exactly he was sorry for, he did not say.

* * *

Amy knocked on Danielle McLellan's door with some apprehension, but when Hunter opened the door, a big smile spread across his face.

"Mum, it's the nice journalist from that magazine!" he shouted back into the room.

Danielle McLellan emerged from the bathroom. Despite the stuffiness in the room, she was wrapped in a long-sleeved bathrobe with the collar turned up. Without make-up, the lines around her mouth were deep and dark, and her dull eyes avoided Amy's.

"I've told you, I'm not giving any interviews," she said with a despair that seemed bottomless.

Amy wondered what other scars Danielle McLellan bore under her robe.

"I'm not here as a journalist but as a woman who cares about you and Hunter. You can take control of your own life, Danielle, but you must accept some help."

"She's right, Mum," Hunter piped up. "We can't hide from Dad forever in this hotel; he'll just keep coming back."

Danielle McLellan dropped the towel she was drying her hair with.

"Why, when was he here?"

Hunter closely examined the tartan pattern of the carpet. "On Monday. I saw him walking along Corstorphine Road when we came back from the shops. I didn't say anything at the time because I didn't want to worry you."

"Worry me? You need to tell me!" Her voice had taken on a hysterical note. "How can I protect you when I don't know about these things?"

Hunter put his arms around her. "I don't need protecting, Mum. He never hurt me. It was you he hurt."

"Hang on," Amy interrupted, "Monday? That was the day your grandpa was... eh, died. You saw your father that morning outside the hotel?"

Hunter nodded slowly, still hugging his mother. "I didn't mention it at the time because I was... in shock."

"Of course, you were," Amy said, welling up at the thought of the wee lad finding his grandfather murdered. But then the sleuth in her took over again. What if she had been wrong about Sinclair?

"DI McCord needs to know about this," she said, pulling out her phone. She pressed a speed dial button and held the phone out to Hunter. "Go on, tell him."

To her surprise, Hunter drew back and shook his head. "No, you tell him."

Amy pressed the phone to her ear but there was no sound. She unclicked the mute button.

"Hello? Amy, are you alright? Amy?!" There was a distinct note of panic in McCord's voice.

"Yes, yes, I'm fine."

McCord cleared his throat. "I got your call, but I couldn't hear anything. I thought you might have gone after McLellan and got into trouble. Again," he added.

"Don't start. In fact, I am with Hunter and his mum, and he has something to tell you."

She stretched her arm out to Hunter, but once more he shook his head.

She moved away from Hunter to the window and held the phone close to her face. "McCord," she said quietly and urgently, "Hunter saw his father at the hotel... on Monday morning when he and his mum came back from the shops."

McCord drew in a sharp breath. "On the day Fisher was killed?"

"Yes, he didn't mention it at the time because he was in shock, the poor lamb. I know that you have Sinclair in custody–"

"As a matter of fact, we don't anymore," McCord said.

Amy forgot all about being discreet.

"You have released him?"

"Someone came forward and gave him an alibi for the time of the murder – the pair of them were out climbing mountains. We still think it was him who set fire to Roseburn House, but we have no evidence, and he has not made a confession, so we had no option but to release him."

"So now, with Hunter's news, it all makes sense, doesn't it?" Amy said. She stopped herself from explaining her thoughts; she did not want to spell it out in front of Hunter that he might have unwittingly put his father in the frame for murder. McCord would understand her anyway.

However, instead of heaping praise on her and Hunter, all McCord said was, "Hmm."

Amy clenched her fist, waiting for him to say something else, anything else. But there came only silence. Why could he never, ever acknowledge what she had done?

"That is very interesting," McCord said, eventually. "Thanks for letting me know."

The line went dead.

"What did he say?" Hunter asked anxiously.

Amy relaxed her fist and managed a smile.

"He said you are a brave boy and a fine detective, and you have probably helped him find out exactly what happened to your grandpa."

And saved your mother from a monster of a husband, she continued silently as her eyes met Danielle's. For the first time, she saw a spark of hope in them.

* * *

At the other end of the line, McCord slowly lowered his phone.

"What was that?" Calderwood asked. "Is Amy okay?"

"Yes, she is with Danielle McLellan on her crusade against domestic violence, and a moment ago Hunter told them that he saw his father outside the hotel on the day of Fisher's murder."

Calderwood almost spilled his coffee.

"But that's exactly what we need, sir, isn't it? A witness who places McLellan at the scene of the crime?"

McCord stroked his chin thoughtfully.

"What are we waiting for? Should we not arrest him?" Calderwood asked.

"Something's not quite right," McCord said. "Do you remember what Amy told us about the time when McLellan turned up at the hotel before the murder? Hunter confronted his father and told him to leave them alone. And after Fisher's murder, I asked his mother, in Hunter's presence, if McLellan had been seen at the hotel around the time of the murder. She said no, so why did Hunter not tell me then that he had seen him?"

"The poor boy was in shock; he had just found his grandfather murdered!" Calderwood said.

McCord shrugged.

"True; he did seem genuinely upset when we saw him afterwards. But he was not particularly close to his grandfather, and when Norval died in the fire, he didn't bat an eyelid. I got the impression he was totally focused on solving the case then."

"It's different, though, suspecting and accusing your own father of murder," Calderwood said.

"I suppose it is. But Hunter says he saw his father when he came back from the shops with his mother, so why did she not see him? And if she did, surely, she would have no hesitation in telling us about it?"

Calderwood had no answer to this argument.

"So, here's what I think," McCord said. "Our Hunter is nothing less than a mixed-up little boy with confusing emotions about what he has witnessed and what he knows. He hates his father for what he has done to his mother. He's a tough kid and he is sensible, and when Amy turns up and no doubt encourages his mother to take action against his father, he has the smart idea to do it for her. He wants us to believe that his father could have committed the murder, which would get him out of their lives for good. And Amy fell for it, hook, line, and sinker. Still, you'll need to add Hunter's comment to our file, Calderwood, so that it is recorded. Nothing would please me more than to pin this on McLellan, but we need some hard evidence."

Chapter 23

McCord had spent all of the previous afternoon, evening, most of the night and that morning reading through Fisher's and Norval's files, which by now had grown to several inches thick. He thought about the three suspects, but in particular about Hunter and his statement. It was obvious that he was missing something, but he was damned if he knew what it was.

Struthers had nothing useful to contribute either. Even armed with Sutton's extended and refined list, he had not come up with anything remotely interesting about the other people who had accused Fisher of fraud.

McCord got up, stretched his arms and legs that were stiff from sitting for too long and went across to the large open-plan office where his colleagues were searching for that crucial witness, that conclusive CCTV footage, that little inconsistency that might satisfy the procurator fiscal that there was indeed a case worthy of a trial.

Dharwan had come back from her second stint at Ravelston Dykes Road. Some of the neighbours had been elsewhere the day before, so she had gone back in the morning. She was nothing if not thorough, and McCord reminded himself to speak to her about going for promotion. She was having a drink from her water bottle at her desk; when McCord made to go over to her, he saw Calderwood beat him to it. He seemed to explain something and then asked her a question. She nodded and smiled. Beaming, Calderwood walked away from her. As he was passing him, McCord asked, "What was that all about?"

Calderwood looked resentful for a second, but then his sunny disposition won the upper hand again. "I have invited Sur… eh, PC Dharwan to a dinner dance."

Baffled at how Calderwood had achieved such a feat so effortlessly, but unwilling to admit this, McCord faked contempt.

"Are these ghastly things still on the go? And you are going to something like that, at your age?"

Calderwood smiled knowingly. "They're great fun, actually. This one's theme is *Grease*. Great music and the perfect excuse to wear a leather jacket. You should try it, sir."

McCord did not dignify this suggestion with an answer and quickly moved across to Dharwan.

"Anything at all?" he asked.

"I think so," she said, bright-eyed. "Nobody saw McLellan there on the day of the fire or the day before, but one of the neighbours immediately pointed to Roy Sinclair. She says he was walking along the road on the day after the fire. She remembers him distinctly because he bumped into her and didn't even apologise. I asked her twice if she was sure, but she was quite adamant that it was him."

"I'm not surprised," McCord said. "In those circles, bad manners are a worse crime than murder. What do you think, PC Dharwan? A killer, or at least arsonist, returning to the scene of the crime?"

"It does look like it, sir," Dharwan said. "It would be a strange coincidence otherwise."

"Indeed," McCord said. "Excellent work. Phone Sinclair and ask him to come in for another little chat."

"Oh, and while I was there, I checked the gardener's witness statement with the neighbour she said she had met, because her alibi had never been followed up."

Here we go, McCord thought. Struthers being sloppy again.

Dharwan smiled as if she was reading his thoughts.

"No harm done, sir. Mr Haynes on Ellersly Road confirmed that he saw Chloe Chalmers both on her way to the golf course and on the way back at the times she stated, but he didn't see Sinclair or anybody else. Not surprising, though, because he is on the wrong side of both Roseburn House and the hotel for anybody coming from the city centre."

"Well done, PC Dharwan," McCord said.

He moved along to PC Turner, who, after watching CCTV footage for hours, was far less cheerful than his colleague.

"Nothing to report, sir," Turner said before McCord had a chance to ask. "The camera above the entrance of the FCA shows McLellan leaving the building at twelve thirty and returning at one thirty-five, but I can't tell whether he went across to Loudons or along the road. There's no trace of him between his office and The Braemar, but the coverage is patchy at best, and if he was trying, he could have dodged it in some places. It's so frustrating!"

McCord nodded. "You've done all you could, PC Turner. Maybe he did go by taxi. It would make sense because he had very little time to commit murder and get back to the office."

"But would he have run the risk of the driver remembering him?" Turner asked.

"Maybe he is well aware of the fact that he is instantly forgettable," McCord said.

"Sir!" shouted one of the officers across to McCord. "Have a look at this!"

McCord hurried over to his colleague's desk. "What is it?"

The officer pointed to the screen showing footage from the traffic cameras on the A70 Lanark Road West, not far out of Balerno between Stewart Road and Bridge Road.

"Palmer-Wycliffe's Aston Martin," the officer said. "Six forty. What do you reckon, could he have made it to Roseburn House for seven thirty when the fire started?"

McCord examined the large map of Edinburgh that was pinned to the wall.

"The timing is a bit tight, and it would depend on the volume of traffic, and the route he chose. He would either continue to Slateford Road or use the city bypass down to the Glasgow Road and then Corstorphine Road. So far, the timings tie in with what he told us, but the worst of the teatime rush hour would have been over. If he wasn't held up anywhere, I think he could have got to Roseburn House in time to set it on fire," McCord said. "Check for footage on other cameras. I know there is one at Hutchison Crossway at Slateford which he might have gone through. The timings are crucial. Put it all into your report. If he was there earlier than he claims, it doesn't prove that he did it, but at least it proves that he lied."

* * *

Roy Sinclair appeared at the station a mere hour later and was shown into Interview Room 1 by the duty sergeant. Is Sinclair the most obliging criminal in history, McCord wondered, or does he enjoy playing games?

"He looks serious," Calderwood said, peering through the small glass window in the door. "Maybe he has realised that it is in his interest to confess?"

"I doubt that very much," McCord said. "I have never seen anybody so calm under pressure as he is. But so far, we've had nothing on him but motive, opportunity, and his threat to Fisher. Let's see if a witness can rattle his cage."

In the hope to startle Sinclair, McCord burst into the interview room.

"Good afternoon, Mr Sinclair," he said breezily. "Thank you for coming in so promptly."

Sinclair did not even twitch. "Good afternoon, DI McCord."

While Calderwood was setting up the recording, Sinclair said nothing but waited patiently, as he had always done so far, for the detectives to ask their questions.

"We have a witness who saw you at Roseburn House," McCord began. "What do you say to that?"

By omitting to say on which day, he hoped to dupe Sinclair into admitting to being there on the day of the fire. But no such luck.

"That is entirely possible," Sinclair said. "I was there, on the day after the fire."

"And what were you doing there?"

Sinclair weighed his words carefully. "Isn't it obvious? I wanted to see for myself the damage done to Fisher's home."

"And did it give you much satisfaction?" McCord asked.

"Yes."

"That is not very Christian, is it?"

"No," Sinclair said, matter-of-factly. "Is there anything else?"

McCord, seeing that his feeble attempt to goad his suspect had failed, admitted defeat, at least in this round.

"Not at the moment," he said. "You are free to go. DS Calderwood will see you out."

* * *

McCord went back to his office, suddenly exhausted. Everything his colleagues found brought them tantalizingly close but stopped short of an irrefutable conclusion. He leant back in his chair and closed his eyes. His arms and legs suddenly felt heavy, and his thoughts dissipated in a soft fog until Calderwood's voice dragged him back to his two unsolved murders.

"Are you alright, sir?"

McCord took a deep breath and sat up straight.

"Not getting enough sleep, that's all. Last night I kept thinking about Hunter and what he said. I can't get that boy out of my head."

"You need to be careful," Calderwood said. "An uncle of mine suffered from insomnia and he died at the age of forty-five."

McCord was not sure if this was meant to be a joke, but he laughed in any case. "Thanks very much. That really cheers me up."

"I'm being serious," Calderwood said. "I was very close to my uncle, and after he died, I kept asking myself what I could have done to protect him. You really should–"

As if he had been given an electric shock, McCord jumped from his seat.

"You are a genius, Calderwood, despite your posh upbringing," he said as he ran out of the office.

Calderwood caught up with him outside DC Sutton's den.

"What is it?" he asked. "What did I say?"

"The uncle. Yes, Hunter wants his father locked up, but he is also trying to protect his uncle; killing two birds with one stone, one could say. But we have no proof whatsoever."

McCord knocked on the cupboard, waited for the croaky 'come in' and made his way inside.

"I need you to check Patrick Fisher's phone records. I need some proof of what he was doing between twelve and one o'clock on the day of his father's murder."

Sutton stopped typing. "What about the other insurance fraud victims? There are many. Not finished yet."

"Leave them for now," McCord said. "I think the answer lies closer to home. Thank you, DC Sutton."

It took Sutton no more than a few minutes to pull Patrick Fisher's phone records, which she passed on to McCord who scanned them while negotiating his way out of the den. Calderwood was hovering by the entrance. McCord handed him the sheet.

"Look! Patrick Fisher got a voicemail from his father at twelve twenty, ten minutes before he went to lunch, but he didn't phone him back."

"Why did Fisher send his son a voicemail when they were in the same building?" Calderwood wondered.

"People do that all the time now," said McCord. "How often have you sent colleagues a text when they were next door to you or even worse, a couple of yards away?"

"True," Calderwood said. "Maybe Morton Fisher didn't want to tell Patrick to his face that he had stopped his allowances, and Patrick went and killed him? But then it's strange that Patrick did not delete the message afterwards; he must know that it incriminates him."

"In itself it doesn't prove anything," McCord said. "And he's cocky; he thinks we have nothing on him."

"Which is sadly true," Calderwood said.

"Let's pay him a visit anyway," McCord said. "If you shake a tree, something might fall off."

* * *

In the car park, McCord spotted a familiar figure that had her back turned to them. Amy was standing next to her mother's vintage MG, having a drink of water.

Remembering Calderwood's advice, he decided to show his appreciation for her efforts this time. He swiftly moved up to her.

"Amy! Good to see you. Do you have anything for us? We could do with some evidence against Patrick Fisher."

Amy, who had not noticed them, gave a start, spilling water all over her sleeves.

"Damn," she spluttered. "Did you have to give me a heart attack?"

Calderwood handed her a freshly laundered handkerchief.

"Sorry about that," he said on McCord's behalf, who stood stock-still next to him, seemingly dumbstruck by his continued failure to create a good impression. "Do you have some news?"

"No, unfortunately not," Amy said. "I'm here to officially report Stuart McLellan. Something needs to be done about that man."

"Quite right," Calderwood said. "We're off to The Braemar to speak to Patrick Fisher."

He turned to McCord who still had not moved and was staring at Amy's wet sleeves.

"Sir?" Calderwood asked for the second time that day. "Are you alright?"

McCord lifted his head, but his thoughts were far away.

"We never checked Hunter's alibi," he said to himself.

"Hunter?!" Amy spilled some more of her water, this time over her chest. "Have you contracted syphilis from your prostitutes, and it has addled your brain?"

McCord's face blanched. "What did you just say?"

Calderwood groaned. "I'm not paid enough for this. What is it with you two? Amy, listen: the boss is not sleeping with prostitutes and never has done. He is upset with you because you could even think that. So, why don't you apologise to him right now, and then we can all move on?"

He looked from Amy to McCord and back, but he was duly ignored. Amy had no intention of apologising.

"What about Dolly? She said–"

"Yes, what exactly did she say?" McCord had recovered his power of speech and his face had gone from white to red with fury. "I'm pretty sure she did not say *that*, because she knows if she did, I would throw her in a bloody cell."

"She didn't *exactly* say that," Amy admitted, "but she implied it."

McCord snorted.

"Did she imply it, or did you infer it?"

"She said you had been 'very good to her girls, especially Candy'," Amy said, becoming more and more defensive as doubt began to creep into her mind. "What was I supposed to think?"

"Maybe that I was very good to her girls and especially Candy?" McCord said. "Most policemen, like most other people, despise prostitutes, but I've always tried to make sure these women are protected as much as they can be in their dangerous business. Candy was raped last year. I took her seriously, caught her attacker and ensured that he was locked away. That's all I did!"

"Amy?" Calderwood pleaded.

Amy said nothing. Humiliation, shame, and relief were all swirling round her head.

"Well, if you don't believe me, please yourself," McCord said. "I'm going to The Braemar now to make an arrest, and you can stay here. Calderwood, are you coming?"

"Of course, sir," Calderwood said, nudging Amy.

"I am so sorry, McCord," she said. "I truly am. I believe you. Completely. I couldn't believe it at first, but because Dolly said... I thought–"

McCord waved his arm impatiently. "If you're coming, stop thinking, and preferably stop talking as well."

Chapter 24

Amy did not obey that order for long. They had not even reached Melville Drive when she leant forward between McCord and Calderwood, straining her seatbelt to the maximum. "You don't seriously believe that Hunter set the house on fire and later killed his grandfather, do you?" she asked.

"That little boy has been leading us a merry dance," McCord said, "but not for any longer."

He fell silent.

In his head, McCord moved the puzzle pieces of this case around until he had them fitting together perfectly. Exactly how he was going to reveal the picture and fix it for the world to see, he was not sure yet. Human beings were the greatest unknowns; one never knew what they were going to do next. Maybe he would simply lob a grenade into that family and see what happened.

Purple clouds, lined with sickly yellow, were gathering swiftly above them as they approached The Braemar. The heat had become a heavy blanket, and it was difficult to breathe. There was a metallic scent in the air that was saturated with moisture. Sudden warm gusts buffeted the tree branches and tore off the petals from the begonias lining the drive. All over the city, people uttered a prayer seldom heard in Edinburgh: please, God, let it rain.

McCord's clammy hands stuck to the steering wheel, and he felt sweat trickling down his back, soaking his shirt. This was not his normally cool, breezy Edinburgh, this was more like the tropics where passion drove people mad.

McCord parked the car and entered the airless reception area to inquire about Patrick Fisher and Danielle McLellan. They were in the garden, on the patio to the west of the building, he was told.

Most guests had retreated into the hotel, but a few awaited the coming storm outside.

Patrick Fisher and his sister were sitting at the same table where McCord had spoken to them after Victoria Norval's death. As he had then, Hunter was playing with his bow and arrow. He was aiming at a target fastened to the trunk of a young copper beech fifteen yards away. He hit the bull's eye every time.

When he saw McCord and his colleagues, he dropped his weapon and ran up to the table.

"I'm glad I find you here together," McCord said to Patrick Fisher and Danielle McLellan, who put down their cutlery and looked apprehensively at him. "I have some bad news, I'm afraid."

He pulled out a sheet of paper from his jacket. "On the morning he was murdered, your father received this letter from his insurance company. It informed him that there would be no payout on his claim because the fire investigation found that the terms of the contract had been breached. Small print in the contract specifically stated that smoke alarms had to be fitted and maintained in perfect working order, but the fire investigator noted that the batteries in most of the alarms were missing."

Patrick Fisher jumped up. "That is outrageous! It's not fair! Somebody burnt down our house! It was criminal damage, and the insurance company should be compensating us for it."

McCord examined the young man's flushed face with interest.

"Well, they won't. But that is not all," he said. "I am confident that we will be able to prove that a large part of your father's fortune was a result of criminal activity, so the victims of his insurance fraud will be demanding compensation. It could amount to as much as six-figure sums in each case."

McCord was not going to tell them that he had invented this scenario and that he was not convinced that those victims would ever be reimbursed. With Stuart McLellan's help, Morton Fisher had cleverly channelled their money through legal loopholes right into his own pocket. Gratified to see panic spread across the faces of Fisher's offspring, McCord continued.

"I also suspect the Crown will want to claim part of the estate to recoup the money lost to the taxpayer through your father's more recent laundering of drugs money."

Danielle McLellan uttered a little hysterical shriek, a mixture of laughter and horror. Patrick Fisher had fallen back onto his chair, white as a sheet.

All of a sudden, the sky overhead had become dark, and a flash of lightning shot down from the black clouds. None of them noticed.

"But there is something that will be even more vexing for you than the fact that there is no money to inherit, and that is" – McCord paused for dramatic effect – "that your father would have died in a matter of minutes anyway. At the time of the murder, he was having a massive heart attack. If you had simply waited a few more minutes, murdering him would have been quite unnecessary, and instead of life in prison, you would have been relatively poor but at least a free man, Mr Fisher."

Patrick Fisher's eyes darted from McCord, who was watching him closely, to his sister, who had turned white.

"No... no," he stammered.

"Patrick Fisher, I'm arresting you on the suspicion of murdering your father, Morton Fisher," McCord said. "You have the right–"

"He didn't kill Grandpa!" Hunter shouted. "It wasn't him – I know it wasn't!"

"Yes," McCord said calmly. "You know it wasn't him because you know who it was, don't you, Hunter? Because you were not with your mum all the time before lunch. She went away to talk to your grandpa, didn't she? And when she came back, she was upset and the sleeves of her dress were wet, and when you found your grandpa drowned, you, like the great detective you are, put two and two together, and you realised what must have happened, didn't you?"

Hunter kept shaking his head. "No," he cried, "no!"

"McCord!" Amy shouted, but he waved her objections away.

He had to get through this, no matter how much it pained him to cause Hunter such distress.

"You, Mrs McLellan," he continued quickly, "tried to cover your tracks by getting changed and putting your wet clothes into the wash. The housekeeper who picked up the bag commented on it, but I didn't see the significance of that at first. Are you really going to use your son to cover up cold-blooded murder? Have you considered what this would do to him?"

Danielle McLellan buried her face in her hands and began to sob.

"It wasn't cold-blooded murder!" Patrick Fisher shouted over the first rolling of thunder in the distance. "It was a moment of madness, and I can prove it!"

Now it was McCord's turn to be stunned. "You can prove it? How?" he asked. "Were you there?"

"As good as," Patrick Fisher said and pulled out his phone. "I received this voicemail at twelve twenty from my father."

McCord exchanged a look with Calderwood.

"I didn't listen to it until after he was found dead," Patrick Fisher said. "I think he intended to call an ambulance and hit the speed dial button instead."

"Wait!" Amy rushed round the table. "Hunter doesn't need to hear this. He's been through enough." She tried to pull him away, but he tore himself free.

"Let me go!" he shouted, ran over to his mother, and hugged her. "I need to know what happened."

"Maybe he does," Patrick said quietly to Amy. "Not knowing what happened but imagining it can be even worse than the truth. It might haunt him for the rest of his life. All this has been a secret for far too long."

He pressed the play button.

Silence.

Danielle: Dad, I must talk to you!

Fisher: Not now, I'm not feeling well.

Danielle: You've never listened to me. I've tried to tell you so many times. You need to help me and Hunter!

Fisher (moans): I can't. Leave me alone.

Danielle: If you don't want to listen, look!

Silence.

Fisher: Pull your skirt down! What if anybody sees you!

Danielle: I want everybody to see it. To see what Stuart did to me. Every day Hunter was away at school. It was you who told me to marry that monster!

Fisher: You didn't have to marry him.

Danielle (sobbing): I tried to please you, Daddy. I thought you'd love me if I did what you wanted, but you always loved Patrick more!

Fisher (moaning again): Don't be silly.

Danielle (shrieking): Silly? Silly?

Fisher shouts out. A thud and a splash.

Danielle: Silly?

A gurgling sound.

Silence.

Danielle (breathing heavily): Daddy... Daddy! Oh, my God!

Silence.

Sound of footsteps running away.

Silence.

* * *

For a moment, nobody made a sound. A flash of lightning lit the sky, followed a second later by a clap of thunder. The storm was getting closer, but no one paid any attention to it. Then a voice from outside their group made everybody jump.

"I tried to tell you, detectives, that she is mentally unstable, and you did not believe me. Now you all know what she is capable of. She murdered her own father."

Stuart McLellan emerged from behind the patio screen, his forehead wrinkled in sorrow but his grey eyes shining unnaturally bright.

McCord whirled round.

"Murder is premeditated, and this wasn't. The judge will consider the circumstances and in particular your own actions, Mr McLellan."

Danielle McLellan had risen from her seat.

"Get him out of here," she said with a quivering voice. "I told the staff not to let that man anywhere near me or my son."

McLellan shook his head and tutted. "Poor Danielle. You appear to have forgotten that Hunter is also *my* son. I have every right to take the boy into my care now that his mother is going to spend the next ten years in prison or a psychiatric ward. And I am going to refute all accusations of abuse; you are undeniably delusional and prone to self-harm. Show them your arms, show them what you've been doing to yourself!"

Staring at her husband with sheer hatred, she crossed her arms defiantly.

All eyes were on her – Stuart McLellan's triumphant, Hunter's anxious, McCord's searching, Calderwood's compassionate and Amy's angry.

"Show us, Danielle," she said. "It does not reflect badly on you, but on him."

Trembling, Danielle McLellan pushed up the thin sleeves of her dress to reveal the telltale scars and wounds criss-crossing her arms. "Here, look, that's what he has made me do!" she shrieked.

"Oh no," McLellan said with a sad voice, "you did all that to yourself. But you did more than that: you also poisoned my son's mind against me. You even got him to lie to the police on your behalf. You are not fit to be a mother. You are a danger to yourself and to the people around you. It's high time you were locked up. Now, more than ever, Hunter needs his dad to take care of him. Come on, Hunter, let's go home."

"No," Hunter shouted, "I don't want to go with you! I don't have to go with him, do I, DI McCord?"

McCord's thoughts were racing. He had no evidence against McLellan that would justify arresting him for fraud; Hunter had lied to the police and, apart from being a child, he would not be deemed a reliable witness against McLellan in a domestic abuse complaint; Amy would testify in court but she had not directly observed the abuse either and could not swear to the fact that McLellan was responsible for the scars on Danielle's thighs; Danielle, having killed her dying father, had not exactly helped her case; even if matters went to court, it would take months at best; he could try to place Hunter in the care of social services citing a danger of abuse, but Hunter himself had admitted that his father had never harmed him. To anyone with no intimate knowledge of the family, it was Danielle who would appear to present the greater danger to Hunter, not his father.

McCord became aware that Danielle was staring at him. Was she reading his thoughts?

"He's not getting his hands on Hunter," she said, her voice low and calm, "I'd rather spend a few more years in prison."

She grabbed a knife from the table and hurled herself towards McLellan. Calderwood lunged forward, but too late. Danielle thrust the knife deep into McLellan's chest, who, with a look of surprise, collapsed on the patio in slow motion. The sky exploded with light and noise, and the heavens opened as they all stood there, stunned, watching the rain pouring down, mingling with the blood on the stone.

* * *

The thunderstorm swept across the city for less than an hour. It cleared the atmosphere, washed away the dust and left everything sparkling and fresh. The relieved citizens opened their windows and breathed in the cool air.

After the emergency services, police cars and forensic teams had left, a subdued calm returned to The Braemar whose manager retreated to his office exhausted, mourning the slaughter of the reputation of this once-venerated establishment. Two constables were guarding both the front entrance and the gate at the back to keep in check the crowd of reporters who were hoping for an interview, or at least a picture of anybody involved in the latest tragedy befalling the Fisher family.

McCord, Calderwood, and Amy were enjoying a refreshing drink before facing the mob outside. In McCord's case, there was also a very uncomfortable meeting with Gilchrist waiting for him, after which a mountain of paperwork would have to be completed. No doubt, just like in February, there would be an inquiry into how a simple arrest had ended in death; but this time, McCord would not come out of it covered in glory.

Ach, to hell, he thought.

"How is Hunter?" McCord asked.

He had not yet had a chance to speak to the boy because he had been supervising the transfer of Danielle McLellan to the Royal Edinburgh Hospital for psychiatric assessment, and that of her husband's body to the morgue, as well as the whole clearing-up operation afterwards.

"Hunter is distraught, obviously," Amy said, "but I think he is going to be okay. When I went up to see him, he and Patrick were cuddled up on the sofa talking about how they were going to visit his mum as soon as possible. Patrick said it was only when he listened to the voicemail that he understood how much his sister had suffered. He wanted to protect both her and Hunter and that is why he kept quiet about it."

"If the numpty had come forward," McCord said, "Danielle would not have killed her husband."

"That's true, McCord, and Patrick is very much aware of that. He feels terribly guilty about not looking after Danielle and wants to make amends."

McCord took another mouthful of his orange juice.

"In other words, you want me to go easy on him and not charge him with obstruction."

Amy nodded.

"I think this tragedy could be the making of him. He is determined to get himself a job and foster Hunter. There won't be much money, so Hunter will have to go to the local primary, rather than Cargilfield."

"I'm sure, he'll survive," McCord said drily.

"But where are they going to live?" Calderwood said. "Patrick can't afford to stay at the hotel."

"They're not sure yet," Amy said. "Patrick is going to see if they can stay in McLellan's place; after all, that is Hunter's home. Then there is the cottage next to Roseburn House. Patrick has no money to pay a gardener, so once Chalmers has gone, they could move into that cottage."

"That's such a shame," McCord said. "She really loves that garden and has already transformed it."

Amy contentedly stirred her mocktail.

"I'm sure she'll find a job somewhere in Lothian where she can help to rewild a plot of land."

There was a hint of glee in Amy's voice, which immediately subsided as McCord sighed deeply.

"Did you manage to ask Danielle McLellan if she burnt down Roseburn House?" Calderwood asked McCord, changing the subject.

"On the way to the hospital she told me she didn't," McCord said, "and I believe her. At the time, she was still hoping for support from her father and for him to let her live at Roseburn House with Hunter. She didn't like Norval, but she had no reason to kill her. She seemed relieved that the truth about her father's drowning has come out; she didn't want to involve Hunter at all in any of that, but he took it upon himself to protect his mother. A good lawyer will plead diminished responsibility, and I think we all saw that her attack on her husband was an attempt to save her son from having to live with an abusive father."

McCord paused and hung his head. "I feel responsible in a way, because I did not give her assurances that Hunter would be well looked after."

"Nonsense, it wasn't your fault," Amy said without a second's hesitation. "Stuart McLellan turned up out of nowhere. We all saw how he provoked her. She felt trapped and saw no other way to get him out of her life and away from Hunter."

"I should have seen it coming," McCord said.

"None of us did, not even I, and I knew how messed up she was. All her life, she felt she was not loved by her father who only doted on his son. She always tried to be a good daughter and then ended up marrying an evil bastard like McLellan who abused her in the most horrific way. No wonder she finally lashed out at the two men who treated her so abominably. But even then, she didn't do it to protect herself but her child. It was a tragedy waiting to happen. Thankfully, judges are more enlightened nowadays about the effects of long-term abuse on people's mental health."

Ignoring her attempt to make him feel better, McCord finished his drink and got up.

"Come on, Calderwood, we still have a crime to solve."

Chapter 25

After a sleepless night, McCord drove to St Leonard's, enjoying the lighter traffic on a late Saturday morning. He was not on duty this weekend, but the thought of the arsonist congratulating himself on getting away with murder did not allow him to switch off.

It was quiet at the station and, sustained by an americano and a bacon roll from the café across the road, McCord was looking forward to some uninterrupted thinking time. However, this was not to be as Struthers appeared in McCord's office bearing a pile of papers and the expression of a martyr.

"I now have a list of all the people who officially complained about being ripped off by Simple Quote Insurance."

"Anything that stands out?" McCord asked.

"Nothing," Struthers said accusingly, as if this was McCord's fault. "Most of them gave up after a couple of letters of complaint, a dozen took their case to the ombudsman, and six contacted the FCA. McLellan dealt with all the cases linked to Fisher, always concluding there was no case to answer. Roy Sinclair was the only one who took his grievance all the way to court. I think you should pull him in again."

"Thanks for your advice, DS Struthers."

Struthers returned to his desk, and McCord flicked listlessly through the first twenty pages of the report Struthers had compiled, but then his thoughts returned to Roy Sinclair. He remembered the man in his cell, stoic and stubborn, unwilling to help himself or the police. He thought back to the visit to his house when he had picked up his bag as if he had been waiting for them and locked the door as if for the last time…

McCord picked up his phone and punched in a number. It rang six times until it was picked up.

"Yes, sir?" Calderwood's sleepy voice sounded through the speaker.

"Calderwood," McCord said, "there's no way it could have been Sinclair."

Unlike others would have done, Calderwood did not point out to his boss that it was his weekend off and that he had a life outside St Leonard's.

"Why not?" he asked, wide awake now. "He has the strongest motive imaginable and no alibi."

"I know that. But think about it for a moment. Sinclair has severe arthritis in his fingers. We both saw how he barely managed to turn the key in the lock when we were there."

"So?" Calderwood asked.

"So, how could he have removed the batteries from the smoke alarms? And from what we know about Morton Fisher, he would never have been so careless as to leave them dysfunctional like that. They must have been removed by whoever set the house on fire."

McCord could hear Calderwood scratching his head.

"Back to Palmer-Wycliffe then?"

"My thoughts exactly," McCord said. "I'm going to interview him again. Want to come?"

There was not a second of hesitation at the other end.

"I'll meet you at Saughton in an hour."

McCord smiled. "Good man."

But Calderwood had already hung up.

* * *

Being kept at His Majesty's pleasure in Saughton Prison had not agreed very well with James Palmer-Wycliffe. His urbane charm had evaporated and been replaced by an unattractive habit of jerking his head to check if there was somebody creeping up behind him. McCord guessed that a posh guy laundering drug money for other posh guys would not be too popular with the other inmates.

Seeing McCord and Calderwood approaching the plastic chairs opposite him in the visitors' room did not cheer him up either.

"What do you lot want now?" he asked, having evidently disposed of his good manners that were probably more of a hindrance than a help in this environment.

"A confession would be nice," McCord said. "It might even reduce the final sentence. Judges like contrite criminals."

To emphasise the point, Calderwood took out his notebook.

Palmer-Wycliffe leant back in his chair.

"You're a bit late to the party. I have already signed a confession."

"Not to the arson at Roseburn House and Victoria Norval's murder, you haven't."

Palmer-Wycliffe tensed.

"Are you still on about that? I've told you; I did go to Roseburn House, but it was already up in flames when I arrived. Did you not check the traffic cameras and the CCTV?"

"They are inconclusive," McCord said. "You could still have made it there in time. But I feel generous today. Let's say, you did not intend to kill your ex-lover, you only wanted to scare her. Involuntary manslaughter, eight years, ending up as four. Overall sentence reduction for full cooperation and saving the taxpayer money and the overstretched courts time. You'd be a lot more popular than you were at Fettes. What do you say?"

"I'm saying no!" Palmer-Wycliffe shouted. "You're not pinning this on me! Yes, I was worried that Vic would blow the lid on it all; she called me that afternoon and told me that she had found out what me and Fisher were up to, so I went there to persuade her to keep quiet. I thought if she loved me, she might... But I didn't set the house on fire – why would I? If I had wanted to kill her, I'd have gone in and strangled her..." He stopped himself, suddenly looking scared. "She wasn't strangled before the fire, was she? Because I didn't do it!"

McCord caught Calderwood's smile from the corner of his eye. He was thinking the same: they knew that Norval had not been strangled, but there was no harm in letting Palmer-Wycliffe sweat a little.

"Thank you for confirming that for us," McCord said, being deliberately ambiguous.

"I swear I didn't!" Palmer-Wycliffe yelled. "I wish I had never met that bloody woman!"

"I'm sure she would feel the same about you, if she were still alive," McCord said coldly. "I think we're finished here for now. Goodbye, Mr Palmer-Wycliffe, enjoy your time here."

* * *

It was a relief to leave the locked metal doors and the smell of captivity behind and breathe in the fresh morning air.

"What do you think?" McCord asked Calderwood.

"I hate to say it, but I do believe he was telling the truth."

McCord nodded. "So do I. Damn it!" he shouted suddenly. "I really wanted him to confess!"

"We'll solve it eventually, sir," Calderwood said. "We just have to keep digging."

McCord patted the younger man's shoulder.

"You're right, Calderwood, as you usually are. Let's go for lunch. My treat."

* * *

"What now?" Calderwood asked, fishing out a piece of Cajun chicken from his summer salad. "Who is left? Patrick Fisher? I can't see it being him. Why would he burn down the house he was hoping to inherit one day? And if he had wanted to kill Norval, there would have been much easier ways of doing it with them living together. He could have poisoned her, for example. That would have been more straightforward."

"At that point, he might have assumed that the insurance would pay up and that his father would be more amenable with Norval out of the way," McCord said. "But we've checked him out and we have no witnesses and no evidence even if it was him. To be honest, I don't want it to be him. He is all that Hunter has left, and he has turned out to be a genuinely nice guy."

"Hang on!" Calderwood dropped his fork, all excited. "What about the housekeeper?"

McCord frowned. "Jennifer Hamill? She has no motive, and she has an alibi."

"But did we verify that? She was never a suspect because we had others in the frame. Maybe Norval was about to fire her, and she depended on that job. Maybe she was in love with Fisher..."

McCord laughed. "Now that is a very long shot."

Calderwood, however, was undeterred.

"Hamill would have had ample opportunity to take the batteries out of the smoke alarms. Where did she say she was at the time of the fire?"

"At the Edinburgh Playhouse watching *The Phantom of the Opera* with a friend of hers," McCord said. "There was never any question of her–"

"Did we take a close look at this friend?" Calderwood interrupted.

"We got her statement; it tied in with what Hamill told us," McCord said.

"But we never really corroborated that, did we?"

"No," McCord admitted. "Fine, you can check it out tomorrow."

After a flat white and a blueberry muffin, Calderwood went on his way home, but McCord returned to the station.

He was sure Calderwood would be wasting his time, but he had no rational argument to back up this feeling. At a loss what to do, he began to neatly stack the files that had piled up on his desk during the past couple of weeks. One was sticking out at an awkward angle and refused to slide back into place: the file containing the transcripts of the Sinclair versus Simple Quote Insurance court case.

There was no reason whatsoever to open that particular file, but despite everything, McCord's thoughts stubbornly kept coming back to Sinclair. And then there was also the realisation that no one other than Struthers had dealt with this file, and being Struthers, he would have overlooked anything that was there to be overlooked. The folder was quite thick, and the contents would take some time to get through.

McCord had barely read the first paragraph when his eyelids drooped. He had not stopped since being called out to Roseburn House almost two weeks ago. There was no point in dying prematurely like Calderwood's uncle, he thought, and he was not getting anywhere in a state like this. He needed a rest. A whole day off, maybe some birdwatching in the Pentland Hills. With a bit of luck, he might see a merlin. He pulled on his light summer jacket. There was still enough daylight for a leisurely trip to Musselburgh Lagoons to see if the short-eared owls were still there. Almost at the door, he went back to his desk and picked up the Sinclair court case file. One never knew. And if there was nothing interesting there, it might at least put him to sleep.

Chapter 26

As McCord climbed the stairs to his father's flat on Sunday afternoon, he could not shake off the feeling that something was amiss. His dad had called to invite him for Clare's delicious Sunday roast, but the brightness in his voice had not seemed genuine. He had news, Keith had said, but he would not be drawn about what. McCord hated social interactions without clear parameters. If his dad had something to say, why not tell him straight away? Instead, he had made a mystery out of it that he now felt compelled to solve but could not, because he did not have the necessary background information. It was bound to be bad news. Maybe his dad was ill? McCord's stomach contracted at the very thought. Losing his father was something he had never ever contemplated. Keith McCord was supposed to be there. Always.

McCord's steps slowed as he readied himself for whatever revelation his dad was going to make, and by the time he reached the top of the stairs, Keith was waiting for him in the open door. His face and lower arms were tanned, and he had donned a flowery shirt in tribute to the unprecedented Edinburgh summer heat.

McCord squeezed his dad's shoulder, trying not to show his confusion.

"You're not looking well, son," Keith said, his face clouding over with worry. "Are you alright?"

McCord managed a smile. "I'm fine, Dad. Just tired."

"I keep telling you that you are working too hard," Keith said. "At least you've taken today off, and we're so happy that you are having lunch with us, aren't we, pet?"

Clare, in a smart skirt and blouse, appeared behind Keith and gave his son the usual hug and kiss.

"Of course," she said. "Come in; Russell, come in."

She rushed back to the kitchen. McCord wondered why they were both dressed up for Sunday lunch at home.

The table in the living room was laid with a linen tablecloth and decorated with a bunch of fragrant sweet peas.

"They are early this summer because of the warm weather we've been having," Keith said.

There was an awkward pause as McCord had no desire whatsoever to discuss the flowering time of plants.

"So, what's your news, Dad?" he asked attempting a casual tone.

"Let's wait until Clare comes through," Keith said, nervously glancing towards the kitchen.

Eventually, she appeared. It must have been hot in there, for her face was red, and she tucked away a strand of hair that had escaped from her high bun.

By now, McCord was desperate for a drink and regretted bringing the car. He suspected that whatever was to come would require a stiff whisky to soften the blow.

"Here she is!" Keith beamed unconvincingly as if Clare had returned from a month-long trip abroad. "Well," he said, pulling her close, "this is the news we want to share with you: Clare and I are getting married!"

McCord's eyes were involuntarily drawn to his mother's portrait on the mantelpiece. Then he turned back to Keith and Clare, who were holding hands. An enormous feeling of relief flooded through him. His dad was okay; no, he was more than okay. He was supremely happy and lucky to have this lovely woman in his life.

"Congratulations to you both," he said, smiling sincerely now.

McCord and his dad, tears in their eyes, squeezed each other's shoulders and patted their backs as if beating a carpet, and then McCord hugged Clare.

"This calls for a bit of bubbly," Keith said. "We even got in an alcohol-free Prosecco because we knew you'd be driving."

Glasses were filled and emptied amid cheerful chatter about the planned festivities in the autumn, and then they sat down to lunch.

"Clare and I actually fell out yesterday," Keith said, grinning, "and we almost called the whole thing off."

"What on earth did you fall out about?" asked McCord, spearing a crunchy broccoli stem.

"Clare doesn't want to change her name," Keith said.

"Why should I?" she said heatedly. "I've had it since I was born, and it is *my* name. And I have my business to think about. Everybody knows me as Clare Hildreth."

McCord knew that Hildreth's jewellery shop in the High Street had been in the family since 1930. Keith looked at his son for support.

"I did point out that she could always call herself Clare Hildreth McCord."

"And I said to your dad, if you're so desperate to have the same name as me, why don't you change yours to Hildreth? Surprise, surprise, that put an end to the discussion."

"She's right, I suppose," Keith said. "Why should she do something I wouldn't want to do myself? It's a truce.

But I'd still rather have it the traditional way. What do you think, Russell?"

McCord stared at the broccoli stem on his fork. He said nothing.

"Don't worry, son," Keith said. "This is not going to come between Clare and me. Nothing is."

Keith and Clare smiled at each other.

McCord was still sitting silently.

"Are you okay, son?" Keith asked, worried now.

"Yes," he said, dragging himself back to the family dinner. "I think Clare might just have solved my case."

"Oh," Keith said, sounding excited and disappointed at the same time. "You will have to rush off then?"

McCord slowly shook his head.

"I need to check something first. But it can wait till tomorrow."

Keith and Clare exchanged a puzzled look.

"I'm glad you're staying for dessert, Russell," Clare said brightly. "It's Sicilian lemon tart – your favourite."

Chapter 27

After a restless night, McCord had left early to beat the rush-hour traffic but was still late after a car broke down right in front of him on Portobello Road. Part of him was glad of the delay, but it only postponed the inevitable. With a little help from Sutton, he had found the confirmation he needed and was about to call Calderwood when his partner came to see him.

"Any success with the housekeeper?" McCord asked, although he knew the answer.

Calderwood shook his head despondently. "Jennifer Hamill's friend remembered meeting a couple they are acquainted with at the Playhouse. The three of them had a chat in the foyer before going into the auditorium. I've just come off the phone to them; it all checks out."

"Never mind," McCord said. "Come along, we're going out."

"Where?" Calderwood asked.

"Back to the scene of the crime."

* * *

Roseburn House had not benefited from the rain. If anything, it looked even more dilapidated now that the crumbling walls and jagged beams were damp and steaming in the morning sun. White clouds drifting across the blue sky peeked out from the charred window frame behind which Victoria Norval had died and shrivelled into the grotesque figure McCord had seen at the morgue.

McCord and Calderwood walked along the path strewn with leaves and twigs that had been torn off the sycamores, past the rose bushes that remained standing proud, their buds still tightly closed. A faint scent of lavender sweetened the cool air.

At the back of the house, they found Chloe Chalmers next to a huge hole in the ground, thrusting a spade into the mud and then standing on its metal rim, using her weight to drive it deeper into the soil. She almost lost her balance when she noticed McCord, but her embarrassed smile faded when she saw Calderwood coming up behind him.

McCord was shocked to see the change in the young woman since he had first met her. She had lost weight, her delicate features morphed into the skeletal pointedness of newly hatched birds and her green eyes were huge. Her strong arms consisted of nothing now but bone, muscle, and sinews.

McCord could not bring himself to say anything, so simply stood there. Chalmers returned to her digging.

Calderwood stepped forward. "Please, miss, you really shouldn't do this heavy work on your own, you could do yourself an injury."

Chalmers shook her head. "My contract finishes tomorrow, and I simply must have the pond ready by then. It is very important for wildlife, you know."

"You've dug all this on your own?" Calderwood asked, astounded. "People normally hire a digger for that kind of work, or at least several men."

Chalmers shrugged. "There's no money now. Patrick Fisher came by this morning to pay me. He was very apologetic about letting me go at such short notice. Hunter was with him; the poor boy was very quiet. No wonder, after what happened with his parents. How awful. Imagine finding your grandfather dead and then witness your mother kill your father. He said he would come and visit me at my new place, but I doubt that somehow. I'll miss him."

She put down the spade, lifted a heavy clump of reeds and dropped it into a smaller hole she had dug next to the big one.

"I had to line the pond with plastic," she explained as if she anticipated criticism from the two men. "Bentonite would have been much better, but there was no time and no money for that. Still, with a bit of luck, there'll be reed warblers here in a couple of years," she said, her eyes fixed on the ground and avoiding McCord's. "I do hope whoever takes over this place will look after the garden."

McCord was still saying nothing. Chalmers stepped on the earth round the reeds and trampled it down.

"How is the investigation going?"

"We are running out of suspects for the arson," McCord said. "Roy Sinclair turned out to be innocent after all. But then you know that, of course."

Chalmers froze for a second; then, without raising her head, she vigorously continued her digging.

"My uncle would never do such a wicked thing. He hasn't even told a lie in his whole life, apart from once when he tried not to hurt someone's feelings," Chalmers said, her voice thick with emotion.

Calderwood turned and stared at McCord. "Uncle?!"

McCord nodded, watching Chalmers closely. "Yes, Chloe is Roy Sinclair's niece, the daughter of his beloved brother and his wife whose lives were destroyed when their house burnt down and Morton Fisher dodged the payout. Her full name is Chloe Chalmers Sinclair. You dropped the surname when you came to Roseburn House, didn't you?"

"No, actually, that's not true," Chalmers said. "When I applied for the job, I had no idea what Fisher had done to my family. It was Victoria Norval who employed me, and she didn't know about it either, so the name meant nothing to her. No one else in the family took any interest in me at all. To them, I was just the girl who did the garden."

"And Struthers, of course, missed the connection when he was tasked with working through the court files," McCord told Calderwood. "I read them on Saturday night. They mentioned that the Sinclairs had a daughter, Chloe, who was seven at the time. But it wasn't until my dad's fiancée mentioned that she would not be changing her name, that I twigged."

McCord turned to Chalmers who was digging now as if her life depended on it.

"Your mother died, probably prematurely, and then you lost your father because of Fisher's scam, so your uncle took you in and brought you up."

Chalmers breathed heavily, both from physical exertion and emotion.

"Until three months ago I had no idea what had happened. I guess Uncle Roy wanted to protect me from the anger and the hatred he felt. It was him who found my dad hanging from the top landing. He told me Dad had fallen down the stairs and bashed his head. I believed that all those years."

Another clump of reeds dropped down into its hole.

"Your uncle must have been distraught when he heard about the job here," McCord said.

Chalmers finally stopped her frantic activity and stood still.

"I'll never forget his face when I told him. He turned white. 'Fisher?' he said. 'Fisher of Ravelston Dykes Road?' I asked him what the matter was, but he wouldn't say. He told me to turn down the job, to stay away from Roseburn House, to have nothing to do with the Fisher family. I refused. After all, for me it was a dream come true: full-time job, rent-free accommodation, and rewilding. There was no way I was going to turn it down. But I could see how distressed he was, so I pestered him until he told me the truth."

"I can't begin to imagine how you must have felt," said Calderwood.

Chalmers nodded. "My whole world collapsed. I was so angry and confused. Uncle Roy begged me again and again not to take the job, and to stay away, but I wanted to see what kind of a man would ruin a poor family for money. I didn't intend any harm at first. But when they planned Morton Fisher's birthday party for the very same day as the anniversary of the fire that had ultimately made me an orphan, it seemed like a sign from above. An eye for an eye."

"You didn't mean for anybody to get killed though, did you?" McCord asked.

He expected her to cry, but Chalmers fought back the tears.

"Of course I didn't! Even if it had been Morton Fisher, that would have been terrible. But for it to be Victoria, who had shown me nothing but kindness! I've caused the death of another human being purely because I was selfish and stupid. I should have stuck to the New Testament, like Uncle Roy always told me."

"So, it was you who placed the cat in the lounge, was it?" Calderwood asked.

"Yes," Chalmers answered. "I had found poor Hamish dead that afternoon underneath a hedge. I felt sick at the idea of him burning in the fire, but it had to look like an accident, and I thought it would be more convincing with the cat next to the ashtray."

"I still don't understand how you could have done it. You were seen going and returning from your walk," McCord said, still hoping against hope that this was not the truth.

"I waited until everybody had left for the party and walked towards the golf course. I made sure I was seen by Mr Haynes. Then I doubled back via Campbell Avenue. There was no sign of anybody at the house and I had no idea that Victoria had come back so soon from the party. I thought they would all be away for hours. That's when I removed the batteries from the alarms and lit the fire."

"But Mr Haynes saw you returning after the fire had started," said McCord.

"Yes, I followed the same route back but in the reverse direction, making sure Mr Haynes would remember me coming back. It was a wonderful sight watching Fisher's mansion go up in flames, knowing that his insurance wouldn't pay out either."

"You must have thought everything had gone to plan until you found out that Victoria Norval had died in the fire," McCord said.

Chalmers pushed a stray strand of her red hair away, leaving a streak of mud on her cheek.

"I wanted to confess at that point, I honestly did, but then Uncle Roy turned up. As soon as he heard the news of the fire, he knew what I had done. He begged me not to tell the police. He said what had happened was all his fault for not telling me the whole story earlier and that he could not face losing me as well. He also told me to use the name Chalmers, so that nobody would make the connection."

"Were you not worried when we arrested your uncle for the arson and the murder of Fisher?" McCord asked.

"I was praying that you would let him go eventually because you had no evidence against him. I trusted you to find the real killer, and you did," she said.

McCord cringed inwardly. Not soon enough, he thought, to prevent another tragedy.

"Uncle Roy had told me not to contact him under any circumstances while the investigation was going on because he was hoping to hide the link between us."

"He must have thought that you had killed Fisher as well," McCord said, "because he didn't tell us he had an alibi for the murder."

That broke the dam. Tears were now streaming across Chalmers's face, washing away the soil.

"Poor Uncle Roy! What have I done?!" She sobbed.

"I'm sure he'll forgive you," McCord said. "He must love you like a daughter."

"I know he does, and I know he has already forgiven me," she said. "But I can never forgive myself."

"You'll have to come with us now," McCord said gently. "DS Calderwood will read you your rights."

Chalmers stood very upright.

"There's no need," she said. "I know I deserve any punishment I get. Can I ask one small favour before we go?"

"What is it?" McCord asked suspiciously. After Danielle McLellan's reaction, he was going to keep a very close eye on anybody who was about to be arrested.

She pointed to the hose hanging over the edge of the hole. "Could I please let the water into the pond?"

"Sure," McCord said, but motioned to Calderwood to stay alert.

Calderwood followed her as she walked slowly to the tap at the back of the house and turned it on. The water spluttered at first, then flowed freely into the black hole. McCord watched until it was filled with sparkling, fresh water.

"Oh, and something else," Chalmers said and turned to the shed.

Calderwood stayed on her heels as she lifted out a large bucket but then he gave her a hand; she carried it over and poured a dozen goldfish into the pond.

"A heron will probably get them tomorrow," she said with a little laugh, "but never mind." She wiped her hands on the green smock and straightened her shoulders.

"I'm ready now."

* * *

They drove through the sun-drenched city in silence. McCord checked the rear mirror every so often, but Chalmers sat with her head bowed as if in prayer. As they slowly made their way down Gorgie Road, McCord reached a decision. He pulled into a side street, stopped the car, and put his parking permit on the dashboard.

Chalmers looked up.

"That's my uncle's flat!" She leant forward and grasped McCord's shoulder. Calderwood made to prise her hand off, but she let go before he touched her.

"Please, don't arrest him; all he did was try to protect me!"

"I know," McCord said. "We're not here to arrest him. Come on."

They made their way to Roy Sinclair's door, and McCord told Chalmers to ring the bell. After what seemed a long while, the intercom crackled into life.

"Yes?" sounded Sinclair's gruff voice.

"It's me, Uncle," Chalmers said.

"Chloe! I told you not to come here," he said. "It's too dangerous."

"The police have brought me here," she said.

There was a pause. Then Sinclair buzzed them in.

He was waiting for them at the top of the stairs, watching the procession. By the time they had reached the second floor, he had grasped the situation.

He pulled his niece into his arms and held her as if he would never let her go. The door next to Sinclair's quietly opened a sliver. Marge, it seemed, also wanted a piece of the action.

"Shall we go inside?" McCord said. "There are people nosing about," he said loudly, indicating the gap in the door, which quickly closed.

Inside, the flat was as immaculate as before.

"Have you come to arrest me?" Sinclair asked. "I've been expecting you to come back any day now."

"No, no, I just wanted you both to have a chance to talk before... proceedings begin. Then we will need a statement from you."

Sinclair wrung his hands.

"There's no need to worry. The absolute truth is what's going to help Chloe most," McCord said. "She's already told us everything."

"What's going to happen to her?" Sinclair asked, his voice quavering.

"A charge of arson and involuntary manslaughter," McCord said, "but there are strong mitigating circumstances in this case. It will also count in Chloe's favour that she came forward and confessed entirely voluntarily."

Both Calderwood and Chloe stared at McCord, who shrugged.

"You did, Chloe, didn't you? We happened to come by to see how you were getting on, and you confessed."

McCord waved to Calderwood to join him in inspecting Sinclair's library while uncle and niece hugged again and told each other what they had been through in the past two weeks.

At the little altar, McCord picked up the wedding photograph of Sinclair's brother and his wife. The brother was a softer and more fragile version of Roy Sinclair, but the wife's red hair and pale skin had been passed on to their daughter. There were still only the two photographs as before, but the cloth was freshly ironed and hung in precise folds over the edge. McCord felt Sinclair's eyes on him, and saw him nod; McCord opened the drawer underneath the cloth and pulled out the framed photographs Sinclair had hastily hidden before McCord's first visit. They were all of Chloe, as a toddler, on her first day at school, in a beautiful white dress at her First Communion. McCord arranged them all around the pictures of her parents.

"No need to hide these anymore," McCord said. "But we'd better be going now."

Sinclair made a strange sound, and McCord feared he would start to cry. He put his card on the coffee table.

"It'll be tough, but you'll both get through this. If you need help to keep the press away in the next few days and weeks, feel free to give me a call."

Chalmers gave her uncle one last, long hug, and then they went on their way to St Leonard's.

Chapter 28

The heatwave was over. The usual cold easterly blew in the streets; jumpers and jackets had been pulled out of wardrobes again and grey clouds were drifting across the sky. Those who had complained about the heat were now complaining about the cold, while most others simply got on with their lives.

McCord and Calderwood had spent the morning putting the finishing touches to all the paperwork on the Chalmers case. Gilchrist would scrutinise it before its submission to the procurator fiscal. McCord had tried to give every aspect the most positive slant possible. As for the whole Fisher–McLellan mess, he had not even begun his report and had decided that was for later. He and Calderwood were about to go for lunch in the canteen, when there was a knock on the door and Amy entered.

"Sorry, no fresh corpse yet," McCord said by way of a greeting. "Give us a break, will you? We are entitled to some time away from murder scenes."

Amy shook her head in mock despair. "Always getting the wrong end of the stick, McCord, aren't you? I've come to congratulate you and Duncan on the successful conclusion of the Murrayfield Murders, as they have been dubbed."

"Go and tell Gilchrist that," McCord said wearily. "He's in a deep depression. The richest Ravelston Dykes dynasty all but wiped out, and the scion of one of

Edinburgh's most illustrious families in the nick for laundering drug money. The press coverage does nothing to cheer Gilchrist up either. Some of your colleagues are asking why a raving lunatic was allowed to roam the city until she killed her husband as well as her father. In short, I am useless, and because of me, Police Scotland's reputation is going to the dogs."

"Since when are you paying attention to Gilchrist and the rags?" Amy asked. "He's always putting you down. You should be used to it by now. My article, when it comes out, will put the record straight." She hesitated. "Here, I've got something for you."

She handed him an envelope with 'McCord' written on it neatly in ink. Surprised, he took it.

"I'm sorry about the whole... Dolly thing," Amy said. "I got you all wrong and I said horrible things to you. I hope this shows what I really think of you."

"I'm sure there was no need for that," Calderwood prompted, "but that is very nice of you, Amy."

McCord threw him a glance that told him to mind his own business and extracted two pieces of paper from the envelope. He read what was printed on them, but still said nothing.

Calderwood watched his boss, rolling his eyes. "What are they?" he asked Amy.

"Two tickets for a sailing from Anstruther to the Isle of May. I thought your boss could show me what this twitching lark is all about."

"Oh, no," Calderwood blurted out, but immediately clapped his hand over his mouth.

Amy frowned.

"What?"

"Nothing," Calderwood said, all innocence. "I've just remembered that I need to buy my cousin a present for his birthday."

Amy's eyes narrowed.

"Nonsense. You are such a bad liar, Duncan. What did you mean with 'oh, no'?"

Driven into a corner, Calderwood reluctantly pointed to Amy's snow-white outfit. "I simply can't imagine you in waterproof trousers and a cagoule."

Amy huffed indignantly.

"I can do the outdoors if I need to," she said.

She turned to McCord for support, but he, picturing an occasion even worse than the Japanese dinner, failed to come up with an encouraging response.

"Of course, you can always take one of your birdwatching buddies with you, if that's what you prefer," she said testily.

Recognising that his outburst and its aftermath was threatening to derail a potentially romantic outing for Amy and his boss, Calderwood stepped in.

"No, no, the Isle of May is ideal for the novice birdwatcher, isn't it, sir? I've heard one is almost guaranteed to see puffins there. Aren't they adorable with those colourful beaks full of little fish? Amy, you would love them. Isn't that right, sir?"

"Probably," McCord said. "People who know nothing about birds always go crazy about puffins and ignore the ones that are far more interesting, like the razorbills and guillemots – noisy little devils they are, and smelly, too – and there are always Arctic terns defending their nests, swooping down and threatening to attack you if you get too close."

Calderwood shook his head in despair. "You're not selling this very well, sir. The puffins–"

"There might even be the odd very rare migrant," McCord said longingly, ignoring Calderwood's interjection. "But more often than not, you stand around in the drizzle and there's bugger all to see."

Calderwood slumped back onto his chair and dropped his head in his hands.

"What's wrong with you, Calderwood?" McCord asked. "Are you coming down with something?"

"No, no, I'm fine," Calderwood said, attempting a smile.

McCord realised that he was still holding the two tickets. What was he supposed to say now? Amy had intended them for him and her, hadn't she, before Calderwood made his stupid remark? But afterwards, she didn't seem keen on coming at all. Did she want to come now or not? He would have to ask her. But how? He didn't want her to feel she had to come if she didn't really want to. There was no need for her to make it up to him. He had long forgiven her for her remarks about the prostitutes. It was all Dolly's fault, the old mischief-maker, for letting Amy think he was one of her punters. Damn her!

McCord suddenly became aware of the silence in the room and looked up to see Amy and Calderwood staring at him. Had he just said that aloud? Hopefully not. He would have to ask her. Now. He remembered watching Calderwood asking Dharwan out for a dance. He had simply asked the question, and that had been it. How hard could it be?

"Do you fancy coming along then?" he blurted out. "We could get a fish supper at the Anstruther Fish Bar afterwards. There's always a long queue because it's so famous, but–"

"I'd love to," Amy said with a big smile. "I could take photographs and write an article for the magazine describing our experience on the island."

McCord's face brightened as the threat of another disastrous date receded and was replaced by the altogether more cheerful prospect of a work outing with Amy where he could show her his beloved birds. "Great," he said, beaming. "And at the same time, you could raise awareness of the serious decline in numbers of some of our native species."

Then his eyes fell on her high-heeled sandals, and he frowned.

"But you'd better wear sensible shoes."

List of characters

Police

Detective Inspector Russell McCord
Detective Sergeant Duncan Calderwood
Superintendent Arthur Gilchrist
Detective Sergeant Walter Struthers
Detective Constable Heather 'The Hacker' Sutton
PC Surina Dharwan
PC Mike Turner
PC McGlashan
Jack Carruthers – Duty Sergeant
Detective Chief Inspector Baxter – Drug Squad
Dr Cyril Crane – pathologist

Others

Amy Thornton – journalist with *Forth Write* magazine
Valerie Thornton – Amy's mother
John Campbell – owner of *Forth Write* magazine; Valerie's partner
Martin Eden – subeditor of *Forth Write* magazine
Keith McCord – DI McCord's father
Clare Hildreth – Keith McCord's partner
Victoria Norval – CEO of the marketing company BSeen
Morton Fisher – businessman, Victoria's husband
Patrick Fisher – Morton Fisher's son
Danielle McLellan – Morton Fisher's daughter

Stuart McLellan – Danielle's husband, Director at the FCA
Hunter McLellan – son of Danielle and Stuart
Walter Rennie – Senior Manager at the FCA
James Palmer-Wycliffe – Victoria Norval's lover
Bill Reid – Fire Investigation Officer
Chloe Chalmers – gardener
Jennifer Hamill – housekeeper
Mr Haynes – resident on Ellersly Road
Dolly – owner of The Orchard
Jimmy – bouncer at The Orchard
Roy Sinclair – insurance client
Mr Basset – witness

If you enjoyed this book, please let others know by leaving a quick review on Amazon. Also, if you spot anything untoward in the paperback, get in touch. We strive for the best quality and appreciate reader feedback.

editor@thebookfolks.com

Also in this series

NEAR MISS (book 1)

After being nearly hit by a car, fashion journalist Amy Thornton decides to visit the driver, who ends up in hospital after evading her. Curious about this strange man she becomes convinced she's unveiled a murder plot. But it won't be so easy to persuade Scottish detective DI Russell McCord.

HIGH HAND (book 2)

When a man is killed after a shooting party on a Scottish country estate, DI McCord gets nowhere interviewing the arrogant landowners. He'll have to rely on information passed on by journalist Amy Thornton, who is more accustomed to high society. But will his class resentment colour his judgement when it comes to putting the murderer behind bars?

LAST TRAIN FOR MURDER (book 3)

An investigative journalist who made a career out of sticking it to the man dies on a train to Edinburgh, having been poisoned. DI Russell McCord struggles in the investigation after getting banned from contacting helpful but self-serving reporter Amy Thornton. But the latter is ready to go in, all guns blazing. After the smoke has cleared, what will remain standing?

SHIFTING ICE (book 4)

After a jewellery thief meets a bitter end, DI McCord tries to make sense of his dying words. Are they a clue to his killer? He'll find out. Meanwhile journalist Amy Thornton is forbidden from taking on dangerous investigations, and sent on a fool's errand. Hmmm. She'll wiggle out of just about anything. Except perhaps the place she might hold in the cop's heart.

Other titles of interest

MURDER ON A COUNTRY LANE
by Jon Harris

After the shock of discovering a murder victim, young barmaid Julia isn't too perturbed because local garden centre owner Audrey White was a horrible so-and-so. But when her fingerprints are found all over a death threat, Julia becomes the police's prime suspect. Equipped with an unfetching ankle tag she must solve the crime to prove her innocence.

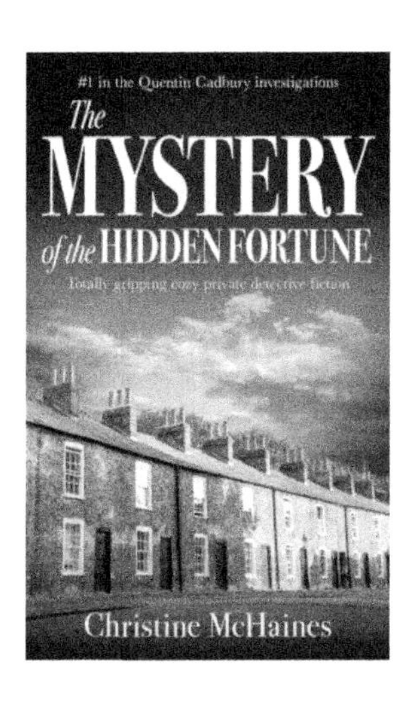

THE MYSTERY OF THE HIDDEN FORTUNE
by Christine McHaines

Quentin Cadbury, a useless twenty-something, is left to look after his late aunt's London house when his parents head to Australia. But burglars seem determined to break in, and not even the stray cat he befriends can help him. As the thieves are after something pretty valuable, and illegal, he must grow up pretty fast to get out of a sticky situation.

THE
BOOK
FOLKS

Printed in Great Britain
by Amazon